REMEMBER AMERICA

Published by:
Gingerbread Publishing House, LLC
www.gingerbreadpublishinghouse.com

For permissions requests, contact:
gingerbreadpublishinghouse@gmail.com

Library of Congress Control Number: 2025948311

ISBNs:
Paperback: 979-8-9997409-1-5
Hardcover: 979-8-9997409-2-2
eBook: 979-8-9997409-3-9

Cover design by Gingerbread Publishing House

Cataloging-in-Publication Data
Vargas, Kathy.
Remember America / by Kathy Vargas. — 1st ed.
p. cm.

ISBN 979-8-9997409-1-5 (Paperback)
ISBN 979-8-9997409-2-2 (Hardcover)
ISBN 979-8-9997409-3-9 (eBook)

1.   FICTION / Dystopian.
2.   FICTION / Thrillers / Technological.
3.   FICTION / Science Fiction / Cyberpunk.
I. Title.
813/.6—dc23
Printed in the United States of America
10 9 8 7 6 5 4 3 2 1
First Edition

For ...

My son, Jesse:
Not everyone wants roses. You challenged me with
1984 and the memory of a nation. Romance is quiet here;
the stakes are not.

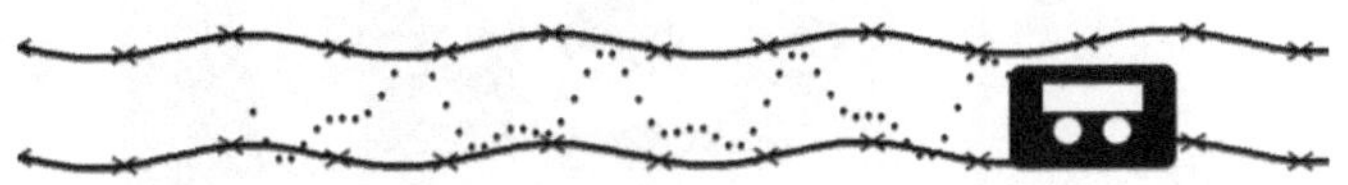

REMEMBER AMERICA

KATHY VARGAS

GINGERBREAD
PUBLISHING HOUSE

CHAPTER 1
THE TAPE

REMEMBER
AMERICA

Elia Ward lived in 312 square feet of engineered peace. Nothing in it belonged to her in the old sense. Union White covered the walls, a committee color built to keep people calm. Ceiling strips shifted tone by her Band's readings, a touch cooler or warmer, always within range. Lemon and lavender drifted from the Harmony Grid:

Seventy-Two Point Six Degrees Achieved
Equilibrium Maintained

The voice came each dawn and dusk, official and final.

At 05:00 the chime woke her. The Band snugged on her wrist and drew its numbers: respiration, temperature, hormone levels, micro-tremors around the eyes. She stayed still and gave the system what it wanted. The numbers rolled into an aggregate. The aggregate drove a prediction. The prediction sets the day.

In the mirror she saw a compliant face; clear skin, steady pupils, lids that did not twitch. She touched her cheekbone and searched for a seam in the calm. None.

Tea: nutrient blend 9A in a regulation cylinder. The Harmony Broadcast rose from the walls:

Equilibrium is the truest form of freedom.
The past is pain. The Union is peace.
Be still. Be steady. Be part of the whole.

The lines crawled across a panel over the sink while she rinsed the cup. Her mouth shaped them without sound. She no longer knew when she had first spoken them aloud, or when she had stopped asking whether the past is pain aimed to comfort or warn. The words did not sit on her; they went through her.

Today her lips missed a beat.

Her Band flickered amber:

DEVIATION

She drew one slow breath to the bottom of her ribs, then two more and watched the Band drift back to white. She did not know why that rhythm came so fast.

She dressed by habit, gray fabric that did not cling, shoes that did not squeak, hair smoothed to the standard the cameras recognized. She checked the vents for dust because inspectors swabbed once a month and dust led to questions.

Seventy-Two Point Six Degrees Achieved
Equilibrium Maintained

Outside, the city moved on schedule. Sidewalks took the pace of the feet. Towers threw back towers. Drones drifted in tight groups, wings cutting air with the Grid's base hum. Screens on corners and bus stops showed approved smiles and open eyes.

No raised voices. No collisions. Intersections without surprise. The Interim—noise, heat, broken glass—lived on posters children studied in school lines. The Union had learned from it, they said. Order required enforcement. Emotion had caused disorder: rage that burned, grief that hollowed, joy that ran off its leash. The cure was regulation. The goal was neutrality.

She walked twelve blocks to the Department of Equilibrium. Silver ribs. Frosted glass. Slogans in soft light:

Equilibrium above all.

Harmony is humanity.

The facade promised purity. Inside, paths turned back on themselves. Gates hissed. Static ran along her arms while scanners measured pulse, gait, and the micro-tics that mark a lie.

A screen showed her record:

CITIZEN: WARD, ELIA
CLEARANCE LEVEL 4

EQUILIBRIUM SCORE 97%

She had never decided if that number marked trust or control.

Down the lift, the city smell fell away and filtration took over. Archive Wing 4B pressed low overhead. Servers filled the corridor with a tuned hum at thirty-eight decibels, a frequency a board labeled agitation-suppressive. Here the quiet had weight. She liked that. No small talk. No forced grins. Work without theater.

Sort. Classify. Erase.

She handled fragments that slipped past the dragnet: home videos crushed by compression, clipped voice memos, screenshots of forums, scans with notes in margins from hands long gone. Most dimmed to static on contact. The bright ones—laughter with an edge, speeches that pulled blood into words—she tagged for Suppression and cleared on the second pass.

The past is pain. The Union is peace.

Pain lived in those files. So did something she lacked a word for. Heat. A room where people forgot to stand apart.

Her queue came up plain: a 2051 family scene, blocky as ghosts; aggressive sports; a line of protest verse flagged for excess sentiment; an audio clip where laughter broke open the room so clean her thumb jerked on the console.

She placed it in Suppression and breathed.

Her screen lagged. The cursor stuttered. Her reflection turned to water and came back. Text flashed in red:

FILE RETRIEVAL ERROR

REBOOTING MANUAL INTERFACE

Manual?

The word landed hard. Manual meant unfiltered and untethered. A door that did not ask first.

A metal crack lifted from the quiet. She turned. A panel above Storage Unit 17A stood open by a finger's width.

Everyone else had cleared out for recalibration. Empty chairs faced dark screens. Lights wavered. The floor hum stuttered. The Grid put its smooth face back on.

Manual mode had no place on today's schedule.

She walked to the panel. Ignoring it would take more acting than she had in reserve.

Her fingers found the seam. The panel gave with a soft click. Dust rose and scratched her throat.

A narrow compartment ran the depth of the wall. A dozen squat rectangles lined the row.

Cassettes. Magnetic tape.

She had seen them in a module called Obsolete Media: Remediation. The tone matched safety briefs for toxins—handle, then destroy. Tape answered to no signal. Tape kept its own time. Tape remembered in its own body. Tape could carry sound in the dark.

Labels in hand-scratched caps marked each shell. Ink had bled into some. Others held gouged patches where names once lived. One stood upright, letters crooked and hard:

REMEMBER AMERICA

Her Band flared scarlet:

ADRENAL RESPONSE

She pressed her palm to the light until it cooled. Jaw tight. Slow breath. Eyes to the corners where cameras sat. The flicker had run short. Short sometimes slipped past logs. Short sometimes scored a flag. The rulebook spoke: report, log, escalate. Clear container to the Chief Archivist. No interpretation. No reaction.

Her hand closed on the cassette.

Weight surprised her. The plastic clung a little, skin to shell. Ink smudged under her thumb. Real handwriting marks a body rose without permission.

She slid the cassette into a slit in her satchel lining. She had cut that slit weeks ago for a cracked book spine and a bent paperclip with no reason she could name. The cassette settled between her tablet and ration pack and changed the bag's balance.

The lights steadied. The error cleared. The console returned to its list:

ENTRIES REVIEWED: 27
MARKED FOR ERASURE: 19
MARKED FOR PRESERVATION: 3

Her hand shook. She signed off anyway.

The lift rose without a bump. The corridor outside looked like a stage between scenes, clean and waiting for the next line. Two junior clerks spoke in soft terms built for microphones: *adjustment* and *realignment* and *time away*. White Bands. She kept her eyes on the seam where floor tiles met. A person could walk that seam and lose an hour.

On the street, wind moved between towers. Even that drift stayed within bounds. She passed Plaza Harmony. Children stood in rings around a faceless figure with a sphere. A caregiver checked small Bands and led a chant:

I am calm. I am clear. I am part of the greater whole. I trust the Union. I trust the Grid. Harmony above all.

Heat rose in her throat, not rage, not grief, a pressure that asked for a name. She pressed tongue to teeth until it dropped back down.

At a corner, two Enforcers in mirrored visors spoke to a citizen with a yellow Band. Their tone poured measured concern from a pitcher labeled Safety. The citizen nodded until the motion turned mechanical. Elia let the crowd carry her past. *Be still. Be steady.* The cassette tapped once against her ribs.

By the time she reached her tower, the Band had warmed against her skin:

Elevated BPM

Activate a calming sequence?

Accept / Decline

 Decline.

Prompt again?

Decline.

The third timed out. The Band gave a small vibration that promised a kind reading later.

Her door read her and slid open. Union White waited without invitation.

Seventy-Two Point Six Degrees Achieved

Equilibrium Maintained

The Broadcast rose again:

We are the future we deserve.

She set the satchel on the desk and stood. Home metrics tracked consumption, not posture. The Grid priced public motion higher than private stillness. That gap mattered.

She opened the inner seam and drew the cassette. The title shouted in silence.

REMEMBER AMERICA.

The shape of the word pressed on her. She had never seen it in a module, not even as a typo. She went to the terminal and typed:

A-M-E-R-I-C-A.

The system, in a mother-safe tone, blinked red:

INVALID: NO SUCH TERM EXISTS

The Band pulsed. She pressed the housing to the desk edge and waited for the light to dull. Pain ringed the wrist in a small circle no graph would show.

Scratched along the plastic, almost hidden under the ink; Listen.

She turned the shell and logged the damage the way she logged artifacts at work. Hairline crack near the corner. Chip along the back seam. Ink smear where a finger slid. Someone wrote the title in a rush. Someone needed the word to exist.

The panel at the sink cycled new lines:

Be part of the whole.

A scenic loop showed a lake and two children skipping stones. A prompt offered a ten-minute centering session and two balance points. The Band stroked her wrist with a light that imitated a hand.

She thought of the archives and the laughter that cut across her thumb's path like a blade. She thought of a rumor in the stacks; Drifters under the city who bled for scraps of the old world because those scraps carried heat. She thought of eyes in a crowd that did not look away when drones passed. Those eyes might someday fix on her and read more than numbers.

Wanting invited deviation. Deviation invited corrections. Correction came on glossy paper with gardens and paths at a retreat where the Grid rewrote minds that refused the plan.

Her palm found the cassette again. The shell warmed in her hand. The reels inside gave a small rattle. Tape decays without care. Memories do the same.

She raised the bed frame and pulled a cassette player from the shallow storage. She had lifted it from an incineration pile in a dead education wing and hid it the way people used to hide a charm or a key. Plastic tack on the surface. Buttons with worn edges.

She set it on the desk and waited for breath to even out.

Light slid toward evening. Vents exhaled lemon and lavender. The terminal held its lake. The system offered points again. The Band nudged her skin.

She slid the cassette into the player. The fit ran tight or her hand lacked steadiness. She breathed and guided it home. The latch clicked. Her heart kicked once.

The Broadcast raised its volume by a small step:

We are the future we deserve.

Elia dropped the room's sound by two taps. The apartment hesitated, then obeyed.

Her finger hovered over the Play button. A shallow dip marked years of use. Another thumb had sat in that place.

Seventy-Two Point Six Degrees Achieved

Equilibrium Maintained

Repeated from the wall. The voice carried no origin. The Grid had built it to be everyone and no one.

She thought of her mother's registry smile, smooth and careful. Then of a forbidden photo—mouth open in a laugh, hair in motion, noise in the air. She tried to hear that laugh without the Grid.

Her pulse climbed. The screen showed a prompt:

Elevated BPM

Start a four-minute regulation cycle?

Accept / Decline

Decline.

A thin red line flashed and vanished. Error, echo, or a small future she would not control.

She leaned in. The brown ribbon lay wound on its spools like a road through a place she had never walked. She drew three slow breaths.

Her thumb found the worn dip and pressed.

CHAPTER 2
ECHO PROTOCOL

The cassette player had no business still working. Static, rough and warm, nothing like the Grid's filter. The noise broke and stitched, then broke again. A voice climbed through, female and uncorrected, as if stone had scraped it on the way out.

If you hear this, they missed it. Or someone like you let it pass. Thank you. My name can wait. Memory cannot. Remember what they made you forget.

Elia lowered the room sound with two taps, then cut the Harmony Broadcast. Vent hiss. A small tick in the wall. Her pulse counted in her neck. Her Band pulsed a warning. She turned her wrist against the desk edge until the contact dulled the sensor. At thirteen she learned grief trips a flag. Pain turns into a form. A form opens a door that does not close when you come back.

The voice cut through again.

America broke. Loud and flawed but ours. We were not perfect. Often not good. We owned it. We are not a program. Not a number. They said the Interim made the Union necessary. They used fear.

Her Band pulsed:

DEVIATION

Her thumb moved to pause, missed, then found the button. The cut hit hard. She stood because sitting felt like agreement. Heat climbed her face. She unclipped the Band and docked it. Metal kissed the prongs with a small sound, her head marked as loud. A red groove ringed her wrist where plastic had lived. Air on that skin felt new and exposed.

She did not count to ten or ask for a centering cycle. She walked back to the desk and pressed Play.

If you live as I lived, questions already leak through. Why your memories sit flat. Why dreams carry sounds without faces. They scrubbed more than facts. They scrubbed hunger and fear. That rage means you are alive.

Alive did not arrive as reading on a console. It struck and stayed. In the Union, alive equals green checks— oxygen within range, pulse within range, waveforms inside bands. You never check your own box. A system checks for you.

Tears rose. Not on schedule. Not for a winter ritual. They came without permission and cut tracks down her face. She pressed her knuckles to her mouth to keep sound inside and failed. A small sound still left and sat in the air. A thought lit with the same hard light as alive: *"I want someone to see me like this. Not a camera. A person with a body. A person who would not call the shaking a violation."*

Static stitched again. The voice leaned closer, as if the speaker in some other year had moved toward a cheap mic so the future could not mistake her.

Peace without memory is not peace. That is silence. They are not afraid of your voice. They are afraid of your memory. Memory cannot be unmade.

Elia stood too fast and hit her knee on the chair. Pain shot up her thigh. She caught the desk with both hands. Breath scraped in her chest. She counted—one, two, three—and could not tell where the count began for her.

The tape ran on.

If this reaches you, you are proof. They will brand obedience as peace and silence as safety. They lie. You are alive. And if you are alive, you are dangerous.

Dangerous sat beside alive and matched it.

The wall panel blinked. Union White sharpened. A red line climbed from the corner. Letters built one block at a time:

NOTICE OF CONCERN:
DEVIATION DETECTED

The door chime hit.

"Citizen Ward, open for wellness check."

Elia stopped the tape. She slid a floor panel and dropped the cassette into the dark with a contraband screwdriver and a dead ration bar. The panel rested a shade off true; she pressed it with her palm until the seam all but vanished. She brought the Broadcast back.

Be still. Be steady. Be part of the whole.

She wiped tears with the heel of her hand, set her mouth to neutral, and placed her hands where anyone could see them. Shoulders open. The posture Human Resources named open compliance.

"Open", she said.

The door slid. Carrow stood in the threshold with two Enforcers behind him. A compact kit hung from his hand. He didn't move from the frame. It let him own the room without stepping in. Uniform pressed. Hair in the approved line. Eyes patient and pale, a second body inside his face.

"Elia," he said, tone light, eyes cold. "You did not report your review numbers."

Hooks in the sentence, hard to see unless you held it to the light.

"Apologies," she said. "I reorganized the flagged queue. A glitch hit. Restore took longer than forecast."

He tipped his head a fraction. His gaze ran a short lap across the room and returned to her face. He read spaces the way archivists read margins. Corners. Table edges. The sink's panel at rest.

"There is talk of a burst from the Fringe," he said. "Unauthorized uploads outside the Core."

He made *Fringe* sound harmless, a stray to be collected. Her pulse jumped. The bare skin at her wrist tugged at her attention. She kept her face set.

"If you see anything unfamiliar, Elia"—a small drop in pitch before her name— "report it. You filter noise well."

She lifted a small smile that expressed cooperation and no more. "Of course."

The wellness officer's expression matched the care icon on her shoulder.

"Citizen Ward," the officer said, "your Band reported a deviation spike."

"My Band sits in the charger," Elia said. "A restore cycle ran after a brief sync error. Numbers will settle."

"Of course," the officer said. "May I step in?"

Elia moved half a step back and held the door space. Not a refusal. Not an invitation. "What do you need to see?"

"Breath and pulse," the officer said. "Band fit. Sleep and nutrition reports for the week."

"Breath and pulse you can have," Elia said. "The rest sits with Systems. I can file a request if you need a copy."

"Place your hand on the meter," the officer said, lifting a small square that glowed. No wires. No mess. A neat device that turned bodies into numbers without any trace the person would see.

Carrow lifted the kit lid. "We can confirm now."

He still hadn't stepped inside. A door frame gave him control. "Hand," he said.

She set her palm on the square. Heat rose through the material. A green bar appeared for oxygen. Pulse next. She matched the numbers to the count in her chest—one, two, three—and kept them steady.

He nodded once. "Inside range."

"Your numbers fall inside range," the officer said. "May I inspect your Band?"

Elia stepped back, picked the Band from its dock, and held it up—strap loose, housing clean. No scuffs. She did not put it on. The officer checked the contacts for scorch marks or signs of a field. The kit's reader lit green when the Band slid across it.

"No tamper."

Carrow's gaze skimmed the apartment and returned to her face. "We saw a content echo. Unregistered audio in this unit."

Elia watched her own reflection in the visors. Her face held. Her mouth did not move. She did not let her gaze flick to the floor seam. "From where?" she asked.

"Unknown," Carrow said. "A node blink can throw a false echo."

The officer added, "A false positive occurs when a Broadcast node blinks during a recalibration cycle."

"We had a blink in Archive today," she said. "Manual came up. The room lagged. A panel popped. The floor hummed. It might have bled into home metrics."

"Duly noted," Carrow said.

Every word of that was true, shaped to fit.

The officer recorded the statement and did not look up. One Enforcer turned his head a few degrees to see more of the room. The second watched the hallway, boots on the seam between tiles, soles set to the approved angle.

"May I return to work logs to align my report?" she asked.

"In a moment." Carrow's eyes tracked past her shoulder. The room gave him nothing: a neat desk, a ration cylinder, a chair squared to the table. He looked down and paused at the faint line where the floor panel met the plate.

He looked back up. "You turned the Broadcast off."

"I lowered it," she said. "Then cut it for the node prompt."

"On brand," he said. "By the book."

The Enforcers didn't move. Their visors held her shape in hard outline.

Carrow kept his tone smooth. "We can close this on a wellness note. Confirm sleep adherence tonight, log a centering cycle, fix the drift. Or we can escalate to Systems and open an audit."

"I will confirm," she said.

He watched her another beat. Silence stretched. He broke it without raising his voice. "Step aside, Elia."

"For what?"

"A quick look at the floor junction," he said. "This unit logs micro-vibration near the desk."

She held the line. "The building shakes when the lift takes a heavy load."

"Then we will rule that out," he said.

He lifted the kit. The Enforcers shifted weight. The room seemed to pull in around the seam.

Elia's chest found the rhythm on its own—one, two, three—as if someone had placed that count inside her and told her to keep it safe.

Carrow met her eyes and gave the order.

"Open the panel."

CHAPTER 3
NOTICE OF CONCERN

Elia's throat tightened. One, two, three. She crouched at the desk, slid a finger along the seam, and found the latch by touch. A warm memory flared—a hand over hers, guiding this exact motion—and slipped away before she could reach it.

"The latch sticks," she said.

"Use the tool," Carrow said.

The wellness officer passed a flat pry from the kit. Elia levered the plate and kept her forearm across the gap to "support the weight." She lowered the panel to the floor and let dust breathe out. The screwdriver and the dead ration bar sat where she had left them. The cassette rested deeper in shadow near the cable run.

"Hands," Carrow said.

She raised both palms. The officer scanned the edges and the conduit mount while Carrow watched posture, distance, breath. He held the threshold and did not step in.

"Junction first," he said.

Elia pointed to the mount points and tapped the housing, so the meter caught contact. With two fingers she eased the ration bar deeper, then nudged the cassette into the channel formed by the bundle. Plastic scraped against metal. She shifted her sleeve over the gap to kill the sound and held still.

The officer swept a wand through the cavity. The display held green. No tool alarms. No energy spikes. Only the building's hum.

"Close it," Carrow said.

She set the plate and pressed until the seam went flat. Her hands steadied on her thighs. Carrow glanced at his slate.

"Your unit logged micro-vibration at 20:16. Home metrics recorded a content echo. Your Band shows pulse spikes. The node reports prolonged Broadcast silence."

The wall panel woke and printed a verdict in clean blocks:

NOTICE OF CONCERN:
CITIZEN ELIA WARD
Equilibrium Score: 84%
Emotional Variance: Moderate
Noncompliance Probability: 7.6%
Risk Level: Yellow
Notes: Report Delay 24 hours
Irregular Biometric Activity in Home Sector
Prolonged Broadcast Silence

The font did not waver. The words held the room.

Elia kept still. Silence struck harder than any alarm. She felt again the clean cut from last night when the Broadcast fell away, a space that fit her as if it belonged to another life that ran under this one.

"Early detection prevents drift," Carrow said. His voice matched the screen. "We offer support before variance hardens."

"I'm fit to work," she said.

"Good. We will verify." He closed the kit. "Report at 08:00. Temporary reassignment pending."

He left with the Enforcers. The door sealed. The panel kept her name on the screen until she cleared it. On the charger, the Band buzzed once and showed a new line:

Equilibrium Adjustment Pending:
See Assignment

The apartment answered with its practice calm.

Seventy-Two Point Six Degrees Achieved
Equilibrium Maintained

Scenic water on the sink panel. None of it entered.

◄◄ ► ❙❙ ■ ►►

She dressed for morning and kept moving. The hall smelled of disinfectant. The lift ran smooth to the Civic Core. At the gates, scanners caught gait and pulse and micro-tics, then sent her on. The entry console posted the assignment in hard text:

TEMPORARY REASSIGNMENT: DESK A12

The chair under the primary node. Full angle. No blind spots.

Archive Wing 4B held filtration and hum. Colleagues glanced toward her path and then away. That reflex told her more than words. She walked to A12 and sat with hands flat and posture exact. The console woke to a cluster of tasks, then idled. Overhead, the node ticked through seconds she could not recover. The room carried the careful quiet of people who know where the camera cones land and keep their faces inside them.

A flagged slogan from 2048 claimed a breakfast ration could brighten a morning. A diary fragment showed as stacked symbols and broken tags. She evaluated, tagged, cleared. The queue emptied and stayed empty. She placed her palms on the desk where any lens could read them and waited. The building's hum paced her pulse. In the glass, distant towers cut the sky into rails.

Footsteps stopped behind her shoulder. Carrow came into view and set a hand on the corner of her console. No weight through plastic; ownership through contact. He watched her face, her hands, the screens just long enough to mark presence.

"Good," he said. "Keep the Broadcast at standard levels. Keep responses prompt. Keep silence inside protocol windows."

The word *silence* carried its own edge now. It pulled at her, a gravity that promised air she could own. A phantom hand closed over hers again, the same pressure she had felt at the floor plate—then slipped away.

"One more item," he said, tapping the desk.

The screen shifted to a new line:

SUGGESTED INTERVENTION:
EMOTIONAL REALIGNMENT MODULE
Duration: 3 Days
Sector 9 Retreat Facility

The text drew authority from the same engine that printed her score. No face behind it. Code.

"We prefer to avoid this," he said. "That depends on your trend."

"I will correct the drift," she said.

"See that you do." He moved on, boots measuring distance in even counts.

The Enforcer at the far door turned his head a fraction and let it return. The wellness officer crossed the room with a kit tucked under one arm and made no sound at her station. The day lengthened without event. That form of pressure did its own work. Tasks arrived in pairs and vanished. The node clicked through hours. She kept the Broadcast at standard volume until the words blurred. She drank water when the prompt told her to drink. She stood and sat on the hour to satisfy the motion quota. She signed the end-of-block form that marked her as present. Every act landed inside a boundary drawn by a system that did not tire.

No one spoke her name.

◄◄ ► ❚❚ ■ ►►

By the time she reached the street again, the city had shifted tone. Screens on corners held smiles past the point where a face would relax. Drones took a lower track and kept her reflection close. Posters told a clean story about health and peace. The air held lemon and metal. She walked twelve blocks to her tower and keyed the door without breaking stride. The apartment met her with its line:

Seventy-Two Point Six Degrees Achieved Equilibrium Maintained

The Band flashed white to mark compliance and drifted to idle. Balance prompts. Scenic lake on the sink panel. None of it reached her.

She did not sit. Elia crossed to the desk, checked the corridor monitor, and crouched. She lifted the plate, slid the cassette out, and set it in the player. The reels showed their teeth through clear plastic. The reels waited. Her thumb found the worn dip and pressed Play.

A breath moved through her ribs and steadied without any program to guide it.

The voice continued exactly where it had left off.

Static warmed the room. The woman's voice came through the noise with the same cut as before—human, rough at the edges, free of smoothing.

They're watching. They always are. But if you're hearing this... you're waking up.

CHAPTER 4
WHITE LIES

Morning thinned the city into edges and instructions. Elia crossed Plaza Harmony on the way to the Department and kept to the curb's measured pace until the statue drew her eye. The resin figure held its sphere high; a seam ran through that sphere, fine as a hair, a flaw that revealed itself only when the sun struck true.

Children gathered at the base and lifted their chins in time.

I am calm. I am clear. I am part of the greater whole.

The sound washed across the square, level and exact. A drone paused above the rings, lens tilting, then slid away to its next measure. Elia turned toward the benches to keep the chant from anchoring in her chest and saw a woman half-shadowed by a post. A nutrient pouch hung from her hand. Her lips shaped one word, barely a breath. "Liberty."

The syllables touched a place training had ground flat. Heat moved through Elia's wrist where the Band sat. A tug answered in her palm, a memory of a warm hand covering hers and guiding a motion she could not name. She steadied herself with a count. One, two, three. The bench stood empty on the next blink. The square pulled her onward with its currents—banners pulsing, caregivers adjusting wrists for the cameras, screens blooming approved faces that held their smiles a fraction too long. She reached the gates of the Department and let the scanners take pulse and gait and micro-tics. The entry console stamped her with a temporary assignment:

TEMPORARY REASSIGNMENT: DESK A12

The seat directly under the primary node. Full angle. No blind wedge.

Archive Wing 4B met her with filtration and hum. She sat at A12 with hands flat, shoulders set, gaze at the proper height. The node above widened its cone with a soft mechanical tick. The console opened a single file flagged for review: a podium frame frozen mid-speech. The face had been erased, the background scrubbed into stripes and stars that refused to resolve. The metadata offered nothing but three words:

NOSTALGIA RISK: ELEVATED

She documented what the system requested, stamped the record with the correct tags, and closed it. Her palm lines glowed faint in the screen's light. She felt watched by more than the node.

Carrow's reflection entered the glass before his voice reached her shoulder.

"The model recommends rest," he said, even and low. "Systems expect a white trend by week's end. Intervention is auto queued; my role is acknowledgment."

He did not add threats. He did not need to. The words carried their own edge.

"Keep the Broadcast at standard levels. Keep responses prompt. Keep silence inside protocol windows."

Elia nodded and kept her posture exact. He glanced once at the node, once at her Band, then moved on. Two Enforcers at the far door eased their weight and reset to stillness. The day turned into tasks without friction. Archived market copy that promised joy in a ration bar. A stadium crowd with words ground to noise by the engine that protected mood. A kitchen table holding a laugh the algorithm tagged as sharp. She erased what the console told her to erase.

She took her hour in the lounge.

The lounge smelled of boiled starch. Screens above the counters posted updates on balance targets and sleep goals. Archivists sat in neat rows and spoke in rounds that never touched ground.

Marlen leaned back and watched her over the rim of a cup. His haircut traced the regulation guide. His smile began at the mouth and stopped there. When her eyes met his, he tipped the cup in a small salute and turned toward his tablemate as if nothing had passed. "Seven point six isn't nothing," he said, not quite quiet.

The number landed on the table and sank. The other archivist pretended he hadn't heard.

Elia's Band gave a soft buzz at her wrist:

INTERPERSONAL INTENSITY

She pressed a thumb to the housing until the light dimmed and stood.

"Neural strain," she said, and the room accepted the phrase the way a body accepts a pill it cannot refuse. On her way out, she felt Marlen's gaze skate the line of her neck and shoulder. More measure than look. The hunger of a man who wanted to sit inside policy and feel taller.

The afternoon returned her to A12. The node clicked through seconds she could not retrieve. She held the Broadcast at standard volume and let the words wash past without meaning.

At shift end, she cleared the final form and left by the side door that fed the Civic Core. The streets pinned movement into rails. Drones tracked lower, mirrors reflecting a white outline where her body should be. The tower swallowed her and gave back its practiced welcome.

Seventy-Two Point Six Degrees Achieved
Equilibrium Maintained

The sink panel offered a lake that never rippled. The Band on her wrist flashed a new line as it synced:

Intervention Window Assigned:
Sector 9 Retreat Facility
Intake This Evening
Acknowledgment Only

She stared until the words stopped being words and turned into a single shape for a single choice. Audit or Entry.

Entry meant time and access and the cover of compliance. She set the Band to confirm.

She changed into cleaner clothes, then unpicked three stitches inside the waistband seam of her trousers and eased the cassette into the cavity she had cut during a different hour for a different risk. The plastic settled against the fabric with a soft click that traveled through bone. She bit the thread, drew it tight, and ran the knot flat with her nail. The player stayed under the floor plate at home—too big to pass intake. She palmed the plate and pressed it closed and let her hand rest there until her pulse slowed.

◄◄ ► ❚❚ ■ ►►

Transit took her through corridors that smelled of bleach. The transport car carried three seats and a camera bubble above the door. The escort across from her wore a face the system would call compassionate. Hands open on his knees. He said nothing.

Carrow appeared once at the dock and signed a slate.

"You will complete the module," he said, eyes level, no rise in tone. "Trend to white and return."

She held his gaze for one count and dropped it for the camera's sake. The doors shut. The city's edges turned into a wash of glass and lines, then into a blank wall as the windows switched to privacy mode for the secured corridor.

Sector 9 waited behind a gate with a seal stamped into brushed metal. The air inside carried citrus and a note of metal filings. An intake officer in gray stood behind a counter that held two trays: one for objects, one for clothing.

"Band," she said.

Elia set her wrist on the reader and let the device take skin temperature and punch marks from the last week. Green edged the display; the officer's eyes did not change.

"Inventory," she said, pointing to the tray for objects.

Elia placed her tablet, her work badge, and the small allotment of credits the system allowed after a compliance month.

The officer logged each item and slid the tray to a locker chute. "Clothing," she said.

Elia set her folded outerwear on the second tray. The officer tapped the pile once with a wand that scanned for metal stitching and contraband. A green blink, then a plain bundle returned: two sets of soft grays, one pair of foot covers, a woven cord for hair.

"Read the door panel in full. Begin on tone."

A door at the end of the intake hall slid open when Elia stepped near it. The room inside measured eight paces by five. The bed grew from the wall. A sink sat within reach of the bed. A panel above the sink carried three lines of instruction. A camera eye in the corner held a steady red dot. Air moved from the vents with a citrus sigh. Elia walked the space once to measure the camera cone. The far corner by the door hinge left a narrow wedge where the lens would strain and still miss half a face if the body hugged the wall. The wedge did not promise safety; it promised a fraction.

The panel flashed her name and displayed the module's opening:

Begin Emotional Realignment Module
Follow Prompts: Keep Band On Skin
Do Not Adjust Settings Without Permission
The speaker above the door cleared with a small pop.
Breathe In

The voice had no accent and no age.

Hold

Exhale

Elia faced the camera and did what the room asked. She breathed and let her chest rise to the imposed count.

Recall a calm moment. Place it at the center of your thoughts. Release any frame that intrudes.

A whisper moved through her head that did not belong to the room. The warm hand at her palm again, guiding a motion to open a panel. A voice close enough to feel against skin. *Stay with me.* The whisper held the tone of someone who knew exactly how much pressure her bones could take. It cut off before she could follow it.

A second door in the hall opened for a group check. A wellness worker led two citizens past her room to the corridor end, where a wall of light asked for posture and stillness. Elia kept to her space and traced the seam at the foot of the bed with two fingers. The seam caught on the side of her nail. She worried it until the burr shaved under pressure.

The speaker ran a second series.

Breathe In

Hold

Exhale

She obeyed and measured the time between prompts. Four sets, then ten heartbeats. Four sets, then ten. The pattern mapped itself. Elia filed it, stepped to the sink, and ran water she did not drink.

A chime sounded and a slot near the door opened for a meal tray. A ration bar, a gel pack, a cup with a lid. The lid clicked when she turned it. The camera's dot burned steady. She sat on the bed and ate what the system gave. The gel tasted like citrus skins and sugar. The bar shed crumbs that stuck to the lines on her fingers.

The speaker returned between bites. **Acknowledge the urge to ruminate. Release it. You are safe.**

She pictured the woman at the bench shaping a banned word with her mouth. Her hand on the floor plate. A face that would not resolve. A voice that lived under the ribs and refused to answer a camera. The module asked for gratitude. She supplied none.

The door opened without warning. A wellness officer stood there with a slate and two Enforcers at her shoulders.

"Check," she said.

Elia lifted her wrist. The slate took a reading from the Band—pulse, skin conductance, stand and sit times.

The officer nodded. "Continue," she said. "Trend to white." The door closed. The lock engaged with a click heavier than a sound should feel.

The next block asked her to name three safe memories and hold them in sequence. The panel offered a list:

Water Under Sun

Clean Sheets

Shared Meal

Quiet Room

She pressed none. The list remained. The module waited, then supplied the set and cued the breath again. Air moved in cycles that matched the prompts. The room trained bodies to be equipment. She let the training wash past and looked up at the corner seam where wall met ceiling. Painter's tape had left a faint ridge under the final coat. The ridge broke and rejoined near the vent register. She fixed the line in her mind the way she fixed routes on foot when she needed a net against panic.

Shift change came with a deeper note in the hall's hum. Footsteps passed in pairs. Keys touched metal in a rhythm she logged without thought. She tested the hem she had stitched at home. The cassette sat against her hip bone, its weight steady and blunt. She judged the camera cone again and moved with the precision of a worker calling out a dangerous lift: measure, step, test, return.

The speaker tried a new tone.

Acknowledge intrusive content.

Replace it with the word Present.

She did not say the word. She stood with her shoulder in the hinge wedge and counted ten breaths through her nose without showing strain. The voice repeated the prompt and then continued without her.

The panel at the sink shifted to a maintenance notice at nineteen hundred:

System Recalibration:

Two-minute Interruption

In Non-Critical Services

Video Continuity Maintained

She read the line twice. *Non-critical* meant water flow and climate might pause. *Video continuity* meant the camera's red dot would not die. She checked the room for hidden fans. She checked the floor for vibration. The vents never paused long enough to test their silence without risk of being seen listening. The notice persisted for five minutes, then folded.

Elia took the issued clothing bag and slit the interior seam of the top with a nail. The thread separated without a sound. She widened the pocket she had carved in her trousers and slid the cassette deeper, then trimmed the thread with the edge of a ration wrapper and pulled the seam tight. The bite of plastic against fabric muted the shape. She ran her palm flat over the line until the cloth lay smooth. The camera watched her fold the bag and set it by the bed. The dot did not blink.

A wellness worker returned at twenty-one hundred with a second tray and a smile that did not touch his eyes.

"How do you feel," he said—absence of a question mark tucked under the soft tone.

"Aligned," she said. He noted the answer and looked at the panel.

"You have a strong baseline," he said. "The module should return trend without complication." His badge read K. DANN. His shoes left a faint rubber trace on the floor and then nothing.

She drank water and let it sit cold in her throat until the chill spread into the chest and pinned the pulse down.

The hall fell to a lower hum at twenty-three thirty.

The speaker offered a final set.

Breathe In

Hold

Exhale

She obeyed. The panel dimmed to gray. The red dot in the corner held. Elia stepped into the hinge wedge and touched two fingers to the trim strip that capped the wiring channel. The strip gave under pressure. She worked her nail under the edge and felt the smallest lift. The plastic flexed, then settled back. She did not force it. She ran her fingers up the wall to the register and counted the screw heads. Four, flush with the surface. They would need torque. She looked to the sink for tools and saw only the cup from earlier, its lid locked with a tab. The tab had a thin spine of harder plastic. She bent it until it creaked and tore it free. The edge left a sharp tooth.

The speaker woke again without preface.

Lights Out At 24:00

Begin Rest

The words filled the room and wanted obedience. She returned to the bed and sat. The Band on her wrist glowed white. She set the cup tab between her teeth and tasted plastic and a trace of lemon from the rinse. She moved to the blind wedge and pressed the tab into the trim seam. The strip lifted a fraction and held. She lowered it and tested the angle. The door buzzed once. The red dot brightened and dimmed. She kept her hand open and still at her side until it steadied.

Midnight reached the room without sound. The light over the door softened. The vents ran at half. The sink panel showed a static field that had never grown a crop. She slipped her fingers under the hem at her hip and freed one knot with her nail, drew the cassette into her palm, and stood in the wedge. Shoulder to the wall to cut her profile, she slid the cassette into the space she had made at the trim. The tooth of plastic held the strip up just enough to take the edge. The strip bent and creaked. She breathed through her nose and kept her chest level. The cassette settled. The strip lowered. The seam closed. The red dot held. Her palm came away with a line pressed into it from the tape's edge. She closed her hand and felt the line fade.

The speaker above the door found its cue again. **Begin Emotional Realignment Module**
Follow Prompts

Elia crossed to the sink, reached behind the panel where the water line entered the wall, and found the slip switch the maintenance notice had taught her to expect. It sat shallow in the recess, meant for hands that wore gloves and obeyed. She pressed her thumb until the edge cut skin and held it there. The Broadcast feed in the room dropped to a whisper so thin it might as well be gone. The camera's red dot stared on. She set her back in the blind wedge, raised her chin toward the eye, and spoke to the ceiling.

"Do your worst," she said, and pressed the switch all the way down.

THE RAID

The door unlatched on a master code. Carrow stepped in first. Two Enforcers took the corners and mirrored the room in their visors. The forensics cart rolled to the desk and threw a green grid across walls, floor, and bed. A scanner ticked through air samples. A wand mapped heat seams in the floor. Every object on the inventory list blinked present.

Carrow went straight to the desk. He ran two fingers along the floor-plate seam and held them up. Dust printed the ridge of his skin. He nodded. The tech set a flex lamp on the chair, angled the beam, and photographed the seam from four points. Carrow pressed the edge and lifted the plate. Empty void. The dust ring stood unbroken.

"Cavity check," he said.

A snake camera dropped into the space and swept the joists. No stash. Carrow slid the plate back and watched the ring settle. He crossed to the bed, dropped to a knee, and sent a narrow light under the frame. Plastic caught the beam. The tech reached, drew out a cassette player, and set it on a sterile mat. Chain-of-custody tag. Bag sealed.

Carrow returned to the seam by the desk. "Displacement," he said.

A wafer sensor slid under the plate and locked to the joist with a quiet click. The tech misted a dust lattice along the edge—micron powder that would fracture if a fingertip lifted the steel. He logged placement and time. Another tech swabbed the desk lip and the underside of the chair for oils and fibers. The wand passed over the wall panel, vents, and hinge pins. Readings held steady.

The apartment watched itself write the report. The wall panel printed it in a clean line:

Home Sweep Complete Per Model Variance Phase B Recommended

Carrow let the words hold. He looked once at the bed, once at the desk, and left without speaking.

◄◄ ► ❚❚ ■ ►►

A door in Sector 9 opened without chime. "Ward. Transfer."

Two staff in gray and an Enforcer with a mirrored visor stood in the threshold. Elia rose from the bed. The panel above the sink pulsed the next prompt for her module, then dimmed as the badge spoke for the room.

"Hands," the Enforcer said.

She presented her wrists. The Band glowed white. The strap on her other wrist locked. They led her into the corridor. Vents breathed citrus and cold metal. Doors watched with red points in their corners.

"Destination?" she asked.

"Cognitive Reintegration," the lead staffer said.

K. Dann walked on her right with a slate held low against his hip. He moved without hurry. Badge swipe at the first checkpoint. A scan at the second. He paused for the sanitary dispenser and wiped a glove that was already clean. A small delay. He checked the slate, checked the badge again, nodded. They moved.

The corridor bent and narrowed. A hatch opened on a room without windows. Steel table. Head frame on an arm. Ceiling lens fixed in the center of a white disc. Four ports on the wall waited for lines. A basin sat under the arm of the chair. The air held antiseptic and a taste of salt.

Ward, the AI said through the ceiling speaker. **Prepare**
Subject
Baseline
Immobilize
Sedation At Count

Elia sat. Straps caught her arms and ankles. The frame lowered toward her head with a sound that threaded through bone. The Band hardened to white. A line snapped into the port at the wrist housing. The wall readout took her numbers and stacked them.

K. Dann stood by the console. He entered her ID with one hand and kept the other on the badge at his belt. His face set to neutral. He watched the frame descend and toggled a filter she could not see.

Breath calibration. Inhale on tone.

Elia watched the head frame cross the last span above her eyes. She found one count and held to it. One, two, three.

The frame paused. Not a stop. A micro-stall that let a hair fall through time.

The Grid blinked.

Lights fell to blue. A tone rolled under the floor. Doors in the corridor slammed and sealed. A foam burst hissed somewhere past the suite. The ceiling disc over the lens flickered and threw a square of shadow across the wall.

Containment Path Beta
Seal Facility Doors
Suppress Audio Variance
Maintain Video Continuity

The sedation arm armed and held. The frame hung over her face. The Enforcer pivoted toward the door. The two staff checked their slates and waited for the next line.

A maintenance panel in the far wall lifted half a palm. A hand slid through the gap and snapped the strap at her left wrist. A body followed—black fabric, filter mask, damp hair under a hood. A small canister misted the lens and left a film that dulled the eye to a gray circle.

"Move," he said.

His grip found her palm and pressed the spot she had carried from dreams into waking. Heat ran up her arm. Her bones recognized it. Her mind refused to name the reason. He tore the strap at the other wrist, cut the ankle holds, and jerked his head toward the open panel. A baton crack from the hall. A voice on the intercom:

Hold Subject Ward

K. Dann did not turn. He entered a command with his thumb on the far key that left a door in the system ajar by a hair.

Sedation Line Obstructed

Hold

The masked man pulled Elia clear of the frame and pushed her toward the gap. "Now."

They folded through the opening and into a service run narrow as a throat. The wall on her shoulder carried heat from a conduit. The floor pitched underfoot. He went first, then moved behind her, one hand at the small of her back to keep pace tight.

"Anything here they cannot be allowed to find?" he asked.

"My room," she said. "One thing."

"Point," he said.

At the junction he cut left, took three steps, then right. A door opened on their approach. K. Dann stood twenty paces down the hall and did not look at them. His hand hovered near a panel. He stepped into a corner that had no camera cone and set his face in profile to the wall.

Elia's room recognized her Band and slid open. The dot in the ceiling turned to them. The masked man raised a palm fogger and laid film over the lens. Elia crossed to the hinge wedge and pressed the cup-tab tool into the trim seam she had worried open the night before. The strip lifted. Cold from the wiring chase breathed against her fingers. She slid two fingertips under and felt the edge of the cassette. The plastic caught on the lip. She twisted, found angle, and drew it free. Weight found her hand. The masked man watched the door and the film edge on the lens.

"Hurry," he said.

She sealed the trim with her palm and pocketed the cassette. The Band on her wrist flashed a line—**Variance Spike**—and dimmed.

The speaker in the hall barked:

RESTORE FEED, WARD

They stepped back into the corridor as the main lights cut to a deeper blue. A drone rounded the bend and halted midair, lens tracking. The jammer on the masked man's belt shrieked and drove the lens off its axis by two degrees. He waved her on.

"Down," he said.

They took the service stair. Boots on concrete. Doors above slammed as the model closed paths. Another order moved through the building:

Seal S-3

Deploy Persuasion Gas

Initiate Phase B

PURSUIT

The voice never rose. The words carried weight without the heat.

A door below bucked in its frame. The masked man shouldered through. Laundry chute access gaped behind it. He unlatched the grate. Hot air moved up the shaft in a steady breath.

"Feet first," he said. "Hold the rail. Slide to the first rung set, then drop onto the mesh."

She slid. The metal burned her palms. The chute turned and pressed her shoulders. She found the rung set and hung, then dropped. Mesh shuddered under her weight. The masked man landed a beat later and swallowed a groan. He cradled his right arm for a breath, then reset his grip on the jammer.

Elia read the shoulder line under his jacket. Wet dark spread across the sleeve. A baton had found him in the suite or on the stair.

"Leave it," she said, nodding to the jammer. Footsteps clanged above.

"It buys seconds," he said. He clipped the unit to the grate. The whine climbed. A warning flashed on its face. He ignored it. "Go."

They crawled into a crawlspace and came up under a grated cover. He wedged it, listened, then moved. Hand signals, not talk. Stop. Move. Hold. He kept her shoulder within reach. Once she stumbled on a rise in the floor and his hand caught her hip. Heat flared and left an afterimage where skin met fabric. She did not pull away.

The building spoke again:

Containment Path Beta: Fails at junction E-2
Reroute
Seal E-2
Redirect
PURSUIT TO SHAFT C

A Drifter in black appeared at the end of a cross-run with an Enforcer on his heels. He looked once at Elia, then at the masked man, and cut across the path to take the hit that would have reached their backs. The baton cracked against his ribs. He dropped to a knee and swung low, buying a gap with his body. The Enforcer pinned him. The masked man pulled Elia through the opening the move had made. She did not look back. The sound of cuffs on bone carried until a door sealed over it.

They reached a service lobby with a panel on the far wall and a lock with a bolt the size of a fist. The masked man grabbed the handle, dragged, and lost his grip when his right hand failed. The wound had flooded the sleeve and reached the cuff.

"Hold it with both," Elia said.

He nodded, set his jaw, and hauled until the bolt slid. The door moved a hand's width. The jammer on the grate behind them pitched into a higher scream, then blew an internal fuse. The note collapsed. The lens in the ceiling corrected its cone by a breath.

Footsteps in the hall. Voices. The intercom in the corner:

WARD, RESTORE FEED
ACKNOWLEDGE
ACKNOWLEDGE

The masked man leaned on the door and forced a gap wide enough for a body to pass, then sagged against the frame. His left hand did the work his right could not. Blood dripped from his fingers and pattered onto the floor.

He bent to pick up the unit. The casing hung by a twisted wire. He scraped it up with the side of his boot and kicked it under a bench. Gone.

"Price paid," he said. No drama. Only inventory.

The bolt behind them slid. The door on the far side stayed shut. A slice of corridor showed through the gap— concrete, pipes, a camera with a red dot steady over the threshold.

Elia set her shoulder into the seam to hold it. The masked man braced the bottom with a foot. Footsteps rounded the corner outside. The mirror of an Enforcer's visor flashed and disappeared as he checked another path first.

K. Dann stepped from the direction of the suite with his slate at his side. He did not look at them. He stopped at a wall panel five paces away, lifted his badge without hurry, and pressed two keys with the knuckles of his left hand. He inhaled, then exhaled, slow and even.

He spoke without turning his head. The voice fit the space between a breath and a shout. "Ten seconds. Go."

The bolt in front of them clicked back. The lock gave. The door jumped. Elia and the masked man shoved into the gap and burst through as the panel behind K. Dann lit green and then returned to blank.

CHAPTER 6
THE CHASE

L ock clicked. Door slid. A gloved hand yanked her through the gap into the service hall. Bleach and metal stung the air. A red diode over the lens brightened.

PURSUIT PROTOCOL ENGAGED

Doors sealed in sequence down the corridor spine. Vents pushed citrus fog. Drones hummed in the shafts.

A square patch hit her Band. Copper threads bit skin. The Band fought once, blinked, died. Sound thinned. No Broadcast. No hand on her breath. Only heart and air.

"On my left," her rescuer said. "Count three."

They ran. The hall dropped into a stair throat lit by strips that steadied and dimmed on a machine schedule. He took the steps in two-count bursts, shoulders tight to the wall. She matched. Lungs clawed. Heat climbed her ribs. A conduit lip sliced her palm; salt hit the cut. She gripped the rail and kept moving.

The door below slid toward shut. The man slammed a shoulder into the seam, drove it back, shoved her through. The room beyond framed a ladder and a crawl space. He dropped boots on rungs, hands loose and fast. She swung in. Metal bit skin. Feet hit grit. He steadied her elbow, then let go.

"Count."

"One. Two. Three." Her jaw unlocked on the third.

A narrow duct bent twice in thirty feet and opened into a low corridor where pipe and cable crowded the air above head height. His palm lifted. Stop. A thin wire stretched knee high across the path, tight to two bolts on opposite runners.

A shim slid under the wire to hold tension. "Pinch here."

She dropped to a knee and thumbed the shim. The wire twanged once under skin. He clipped the line, taped both ends, and reseated the cut between clamps so tension read true. A press. No echo. "Move."

A hover-orb nosed into view at the far bend, lens slit tracking pressure gradients. Paste smeared across her cheekbones and neck, cold on skin; he smeared his own. The orb panned and drifted on, sensors blind to heat it should find.

"Grid maps by movement," he said. "Shoulders narrow. No sudden turns. Left foot crosses in front on corners."

They slipped through a curtain of mesh wired to a rusted frame. Spark pitted the edge. The frame killed stray signal. A chalk mark waited on the wall beyond: two short, one long. Two fingers tapped it. "Swept."

A hand-crank coil sat in a drain cup under a grate. He spun it with a small key. A diode blinked on his cuff. Pulse read, he moved.

Four mouths opened at the next junction. One lip dripped condensation. Another breathed warm air. He chose the cold mouth. Elia matched his cadence and counted under breath. Three steps, then three more.

A ping touched the air near his wrist. He checked the cuff, thumbed it dark. "Cloaked eyes in the hall."

Metallic dust flared from his fingers and hung. Two pale spheres took shape near the ceiling. He snapped a spike. White bloomed on the nearest orb; it spun once and fell smoking into a drain. The second slid toward a vent slot. He threw again and missed by a hand. The orb vanished.

"They saw us," Elia said.

"They saw disturbance. Enough. Move."

A mineral-crusted ramp dropped them toward a perpendicular shaft. A drone crossed and paused. He pressed her into a recess. The drone tasted airflow, read nothing, glided on.

Her fingers shook. He folded her hand around the rail. "Grip and breathe."

"Why pull me out?"

"Sector 9 queued erase."

"You don't know me."

"I know that room." His chin tipped down the hall. "On my left."

Pace set. She matched. Three bends led to a utility niche: dead sink, open wiring panel, floor drain with black water stalled in the throat. The headlamp dimmed half a turn; dark took the corners.

A squeeze tube rinsed the cut. Sealant closed the break. A strip locked it. "Drink." A cup met her hand. "In. Hold. Three. Out."

She rode the count down. Chest grind eased. His eyes tracked shoulders and door seam. His whole body listened.

A pop in the wall. A run of clicks. Two doors above sealed, one below. "We move."

A waist-high cable bundle forced a crawl. Concrete gave to a low run with rusted rungs set into the wall. He climbed first, shouldered a hatch. It stuck, then gave. Cold air sheeted in. He dropped and caught the hatch with a hip to kill the slam.

The chamber held dead switchgear, a row of ceramic insulators, a floor pit of broken housings. He pried open a rusted panel. Inside, a shortwave relay blinked weak green. A lead clipped from his cuff to the pad. He rolled a dial. The cuff flashed three long, two short, then flat.

"Batch flag," he said. "Not a name."

"What does that mean?"

"You sit in a watched group. No personal order yet. Patrols sweep patterns, not a straight line to you."

"How do I keep it that way?"

"Don't hand the model a fourth match. Batch turns to name when streams agree—Band spike, Broadcast silence, intake ping, camera dwell, access tug, node echo. Tonight you hit three. The jammer cut one. We keep the count down."

"What buys time?"

"Band stays dark. No home door. No plaza nodes. No lifts. East tunnels only. Fewer cameras. We move before the model updates."

"How long does the window hold?"

"Hours, not days. Retrain cycles close it. We stay ahead."

Ash scraped from a cold tray. Two lines took shape under his thumb—one short and thick, one long and thin.

"South," he said, tapping the short arrow. "Heavy scan. Faster. East," a tap to the long line, "deeper cover. Longer."

"East."

Ash wiped, he stood. "We do not linger."

Dull metal squares studded the concrete ahead.

"Sound plates," he said. "Wrong step pings a reader."

"Where do I step?"

"Bolt lines only." He pointed to the four dark studs at each corner. "Toe on near studs, heel on far. No mid-plate. No slide."

He moved first, feet to studs, weight clean. She mirrored him across three plates, breath tight, arms close. One plate flexed a millimeter. Two fingers lifted. Freeze. Reset. Studs found. Run cleared.

Heat pushed across the hall from a cross-duct. He skimmed the edge of the pressure field and waved her through the same margin. An exit hatch waited with a lock plate scorched by an old job. A thin wedge slid into the seam, tested for bite, lifted a fraction. Air shifted enough to carry hinge noise. He set his shoulder. "Take the weight."

She braced the slab. They eased it open and dropped into a culvert. Cool air slid along concrete. Water ticked in a sump. City hum thinned.

"Is this a safehouse?" Elia asked.

"A pause, not a safehouse. A safehouse has gate watch, two exits, a burn plan. I won't burn one on a batch flag. If your name prints, we use one."

"Why not now?"

"The sweep could map our entry. I don't lead them to a door other people need."

A match scraped. Flame cupped in his hand. Dry packaging and a strip from his sleeve fed it. Heat rose. A cup met her hand again. "Drink."

Hands steadied on the second swallow. His eyes checked hers and then the mouth of the culvert. A small light blinked on his cuff; he covered it with his palm.

"Batch moves slow. We go on full dark."

"They will mark me dead if I run."

"They will empty you if you stay."

Wind pulled a thin line across the culvert mouth. A drone turned in the channel. He waited for the tone to level, smothered the flame with wet stones, left one warm ember under rock to keep ground temp honest.

"You keep using three," she said.

"It works."

"Why keep me on your left?"

"Angles. Your right foot lands heavy when you sprint."

"You learned that fast."

"I learn what keeps us standing."

He tugged the wrap once more. "Run longer?"

"Yes."

"We go then."

They slid into a service trench under a rail bed. Gravel grated under soles. A mesh flap hung on anchor screws; he lifted it and waved her through. The curtain broke scans. Two clips locked the edge so the frame wouldn't rattle.

An old conduit vault sagged under coils draped from hooks and pooled on the floor. His boot cleared loops for her path. Silence took his mouth. Counting took the rest of him.

A ladder rose to a locked grate on the right. He ignored it and took the left where air cooled and water spoke. Stone caught his finger. "Step there. Not on the slick."

She set her foot where he pointed. Weight forward. Breath on the count. Three in. Hold. Three out.

A maintenance door at the end opened on a palm-width seam. Two picks rolled the cylinder quiet. Latch released. Draft tested the gap. His hand lifted, palm open. Wait.

Soft soles crossed beyond. Two sets. He held still until the air lost the tread. The door swung and they slid through.

Bare studs and a concrete trough filled the next room. A sleep-target poster peeled off a wall; the words meant nothing here. A panel popped from the trough. A small coil waited inside, wired to a pad. Two short pulses went out. Answer came slow. A nod. "Drains read clear east."

Brick took over past the next bend. Flares of old paint showed through grime. His fingernail picked a seam; mortar flaked. He let it be.

"Your steps tell a camera you grew up here," she said.

"I grew up under cameras."

"Same as me."

"Not the same. Different angle. Different instruction."

"You talk in puzzles."

"I talk to keep us moving."

Another culvert yawned. A thin sheen caught cuff light; he hugged dry wall. "Coolant leak. Keep to the dry."

Steam bled from a valve with a thin hiss. His hand timed the bursts. He waved her through on the off beat and followed on the next.

"Why pull me out?" she said again.

"Because that room cuts who you are. I change it when I can."

"You do that for everyone?"

"No."

"Then why me?"

A strap got one notch tighter. "In. Hold. Three. Out."

The old substation crouched behind a buckled door. A breaker cabinet sagged open. A prong met a pad; power bled into his cuff. Three long. Flat. "Batch holds. We keep the long route."

"Who taught you this?"

"People who kept me walking."

"Do you trust them?"

"I trust tasks. I trust hands that hold when walls move."

Her gaze fell to his hands—scar across a knuckle, oil ground into the lines.

A micro-gimbal camera perched on a bracket at the next turn, lens forward. No diode. No sound. His fingers toyed with a spike, then stilled. "Bypass."

A ragged oval cut by a patch crew opened a side path. They slithered through gypsum dust into a newer run. Painted arrows pointed the wrong way—dead directions from an old plan. He ignored them.

Legs shook in earnest now. A gel pack hit her tongue; salt and glucose snapped vision clear. She kept to his left.

A small chamber offered a concrete bench and a rusted grate floor. Coins hung on a wire. He brushed the wire; a dull ring answered. "Safe."

"You string those wires?"

"Someone did. I reset when I pass."

His cuff pulsed two short, one long, then stopped. The lead clipped back to his belt. "Window closes soon."

"Then stop talking."

No smile. Movement.

A collapsed section showed rebar ribs. He tested the span and crossed with a long step to the solid edge. She followed clean. Chalk marked rebar for anyone behind.

Heat pressed from the right-hand wall; a boiler plant ran above. He guided her along the cool side where mortar held. The wrap stayed sealed. Blood dried under the strip.

"Can you run the next two hundred?"

"Yes."

"Then run."

They ran. The hall bent. City sounds dropped from low to lower. Poured concrete turned to old tile and back again. A hatch gave to a pick. He pushed it six inches and checked. Not street—an empty service bay, maintenance bot under a tarp, bins of cleaning rods.

They crossed the bay, slipped through a second hatch, dogged the handle.

Stillness. A hand lifted. Freeze. Something moved in the duct above—too small for a drone, too random for boots. He waited. The sound drifted. Hand dropped.

"East again."

She set her foot where he set his. No mesh at the next turn. Dust shook into the air. No spheres traced. They moved.

A low throat sagged from old flood. His palm found a live line thrumming behind concrete. Two steps to the side avoided a shallow conduit. She mirrored him.

"You keep me on your left," she said.

"I keep you where my hand finds your shoulder fast."

Her breath matched his. On the third count her shoulders dropped a fraction. His eyes marked it; his head turned back to the hall.

Ten breaths on a culvert lip. A small flame heated water to blood-warm. The cup returned to her hands. She drank. The last drops drained. A torn strip of shirt wiped the rim dry.

"When we move again," he said, "we edge a flood channel two blocks, cut under a sub-grid office, up through a shaft into a storage bay. We hold while I scan the next band of doors."

"And then?"

"East until the ground lifts. Then down again."

"You trust that?"

"I trust routes I've walked. I adjust when the Grid moves."

The cup set down without sound. Flame smothered. Stones slid to bury the last heat. Concrete took it and let it fade.

He rose to the culvert mouth and flattened his hand over the flow of air. No move for a long breath. A fraction turn toward her. "Stay on my left. Match my steps."

She stepped in beside him.

A drone hummed down a branch and paused at an intersection. Its beam knifed the air. Dust hung suspended. He read the angle and eased them into a shadow the beam couldn't reach. White slid past. Hum drifted away.

"Go."

They ran again. Slab turned slick. His hand found her forearm and steered to grip points in the aggregate. Slick cleared. Pace lifted.

"Will they stop?"

"They don't stop. They choose targets."

"What am I now?"

"A target if you slow. A person if you move."

Movement took them to a fork of three. He chose the cooler run. The door at the end sat on a soft latch and he eased it open just enough to see inside. As the gap widened, the room revealed itself with rows of metal racks, a ladder bolted into the far wall, and shadows gathered above.

They slid in. Door shut. Stillness set.

Footsteps crossed outside. A key turned two doors down. A low voice moved and ended. Silence returned.

"Next run ends loud," he said. "Breathe through noise. Don't change stride when it hits."

"What noise?"

"Sirens. Old. Not for us. Grid test cycle."

He took the ladder. She followed. A hatch lifted to a dark bay with crates. He nudged a corner crate to wedge the hatch, shut it, and set the crate back. A vent grille unhooked on two clips. Dust puffed. He waved it off and climbed through. She came after. Clips hooked back.

A glance at his cuff. One long blink. Flat. His finger pointed to her chest. "Count."

She counted. Siren rose and fell in a slow arc that stole distance. Steps held. Shoulders set. Jaw held.

The siren wound down. A small nod. "Good."

"You keep saying that."

"You keep earning it."

One flight down. A concrete throat with bars fixed to keep conduit from sagging. He ducked and slipped through clean. She copied. A drone drifted by an opening and moved on. A corner mirror showed no reflection of them. A spike kissed an orb just above head height, pulsed, dropped dead. The spike slid back into his pouch. One left.

The last culvert before the flood channel waited. He kneeled and read the floor—boot marks, shifted grit, threads on a screw. Nothing fresh. His palm flattened on the wall. Vibration. "Lift pumps. We time the cycle."

"How?"

"Count the hum rise. Three between peaks. We go on the drop."

Hum rolled the duct. On three he tapped her wrist. They moved on the drop, ran under the pumps before noise swelled. Sound covered steps. Hot air pushed across skin and clipped heat cameras for a breath. Shadow took them. The cycle peaked, ebbed, slid away.

He listened. No steps near. No drone tone close.

"We rest," he said. "Batch flag holds for hours. We move at dark."

Gloves came off first. Then the mask straps. He eased the rig down and set it beside the cup. A face came into view—scar through one brow, jaw rough with a day's growth, eyes green and alert. Heat lived in the work lines across his knuckles.

Elia stared before she could stop it.

"What?" he asked.

"You look familiar."

He studied her for a breath, then glanced to the corridor mouth and back. "Why Sector 9? Start to finish."

"Notice of Concern at home. I cut the Broadcast. A node blink logged it. 'Intervention auto queued.' Wellness intake."

"Chain prints erase," he said. Eyes stayed on hers until she nodded. He fed the flame, passed her the cup. "Drink."

Warmth steadied her hands on the second swallow.

He checked her wrap, tugged the strip once. "Elia, count again. In. Hold. Three. Out."

Her gaze snapped up. "You know my name."

"You said it at intake," he said too quickly, then looked away to the tunnel mouth.

She let the silence hang. "Well. You know mine. What's yours?"

"Zane."

She held the name, tested it against the shape in memory that refused to form. Recognition did not move.

Her fingers found her pocket. The cassette settled into her palm. Crooked ink—REMEMBER AMERICA—caught the firelight. Scuffs showed. A hairline crack ran through the R. Static rose inside her head. A rough voice followed:

If you're hearing this... you're waking up.

Zane watched her hands and said nothing.

She slid the tape back into the pocket. "I'm not giving this to anyone."

"Good."

"Good?"

"If they find plastic, they call it safety and burn it," he said, voice dropped. "If they learn you heard it, they don't stop at plastic."

He smothered the flame, left one ember under stone, stood, and pulled the mask back up without sealing it.

"They'll erase you."

"Not tonight," she said.

He checked his cuff. "Full dark in two minutes."

"Then we move."

"Stay on my left. Match my steps." Fingers lifted. "One. Two. Three."

CHAPTER 7
THE DRIFTERS

They moved under cover of darkness, skirting the husk of the Old Metro Lines, shattered tunnels buried beneath decades of sanctioned silence. Elia had seen the blueprints once in a sanitized archive sheet. The Union had marked the network *nonfunctional* and *culturally irrelevant*, as if neglect could be a kind of moral, as if a map could outlaw a place.

But the maps lied.

Their breath made small clouds in the cold. Footfalls hushed on damp concrete. Zane kept an even pace a few strides ahead, his lamp a thin coin that skimmed pipes and cables and the ghost curve of tile where a station name had been scraped to bone. At the edge of Sector 19 they stopped before a wall the color of old teeth, its surface stamped with a faded Union seal:

PROPERTY OF THE HARMONY AUTHORITY MAINTENANCE ACCESS PROHIBITED

Zane set his palm flat to the stone. For a heartbeat nothing happened. Then a click, a throat clearing. A seam Elia would have sworn didn't exist exhaled dust. A panel slid sideways with a long, impatient sigh.

Light spilled out.

Not the cold fluorescence of the city above. No calibrated lumens. No algorithmic temperature. Warm flickering gold. It smelled of heat and smoke and cooked food and wool and iron. The smell of life. People lived here and had not asked permission.

Zane looked back. "Keep your hood up," he said. "Eyes open. Mouth shut."

She nodded, though the air pouring from the seam made her want to breathe with her mouth wide as a child at a carnival. The hunger for it embarrassed her.

They went in.

The corridor narrowed, then widened into a chamber so large Elia's breath caught. The old transfer station's bones still showed—the soaring arch, the octagonal pillars—but the Drifters had clothed it in salvage and color. Curtains sewn from rags draped the walls, seams stitched in careful, stubborn patterns. Hand-painted words looped along columns in uneven letters: *Resist. Question. Feel.* Someone had painted an eye on one pillar, not the Union's cool diamond iris but a human eye, bloodshot and laughing.

Shelves cobbled from pallets and pipelined the perimeter, bowed under books and broken tablets and cracked frames that held paper people had decided mattered: handwritten recipes, a child's lopsided bird, a ticket stub dated with a year the Union didn't admit existed. Screens scavenged from dead terminals flickered with old-world footage on a loop—forest canopies from below, waves shouldering a dark pier, people laughing into a wind that tangled their hair.

Bodies moved through it all, thirty at least, maybe more. Men and women and teenagers. Some with synthetic limbs scuffed by use. Others with scars unhidden on throat and brow and forearm. No uniforms. No Bands. No Harmony Broadcast. The sound was not quiet; it was low and human, voices threaded through with the clatter of metal and the clink of crockery and the sigh of fabric being shaken out and folded.

They saw Zane and did not cheer. They did not smile big and false or lift hands for a scripted greeting. They looked. They weighed. Attention moved over Elia like water over rock—cool and steady, searching for cracks.

Zane lifted a hand. "She's not one of them," he said, voice pitched to carry without a shout. "She found it."

A figure stepped forward from the near side of the chamber. Dark skin. Silver threaded through tight braids.

Hawk eyes that took the whole and then the parts—the way you study a bomb or a baby. Patched jacket zipped to the throat. Fingerless gloves.

"She brought the tape?" the woman asked.

"I have it," Elia said. Her hand pressed her pocket without meaning to; fingers tightened until fabric creaked.

The woman's face did not soften. "We've lost people to ghosts," she said. "Don't make us bleed for nothing."

Elia met that look because looking away would be worse. "It's real," she said. "I've listened."

The air shifted. Not a movement so much as a redistribution of attention, a sound inside a sound, the way a congregation leans as one body when the preacher lifts his hands.

The woman nodded once. "I'm Mireya," she said. "I run this station. For now."

Zane's mouth slanted. "She doesn't need an interrogation."

"I'm not interrogating," Mireya said, the smallest curve of humor moving through the words—so thin Elia might have imagined it. "I'm protecting the last thing the Union hasn't turned into a pill." She pointed at the drapes and shelves buckled with paper and the screens playing old rain. "Memory."

A man in a gray jacket stepped to her shoulder— doorframe-still, wellness cadence without the lie. Sector 9 lived in his posture; the eyes had crossed to the other side. A small ring caught light at his nostril.

"Kade," Zane said.

"Sector 9 circulates decoys," Kade said. "Assume plant until disconfirmed."

Mireya lifted two fingers. Kade went quiet, gaze still counting.

"Come," she said to Elia. "Eat, then talk. In that order. People die here when we forget the order of things."

They ushered Elia toward a line of battered bowls. Steam rose from a pot the size of a barrel—lentils and carrots and something green. The smell was plain and miraculous. A woman with a toddler on her hip ladled stew and set a chipped cup beside it. "Water's clean," she said. "Not from the pipes. From rain."

Elia carried the bowl to a corner of the station that had once been a maintenance room and was now a room only because it had a door. A low table. Two crates for seats. A rolled blanket in the corner. Zane slid in a breath later and lowered himself onto the opposite crate with the kind of care that meant something hurt.

She glanced at his ribs. "You okay?"

"I've had worse," he said. "They aimed low this time."

The stew scalded her tongue. She didn't care. It was bland, and the blandness felt like a proof—a taste that had not been improved into nothing. She ate with the concentration of someone relearning an old thing. Zane watched, not admiring and not mocking. Cataloguing. She realized she liked the attention only because it didn't come with instructions attached.

"They all live here?" she asked when the bowl was half empty.

"Some," Zane said. "Others rotate through, bring news, take medicine, swap parts. Most stay until the model sniffs too close."

"And you trust all of them?" She heard the Union in the question and hated it, but she wanted the answer.

"No," he said. "Trust isn't the currency here." He tapped his knuckles against his sternum. "Belief is. That we exist. That memory matters. That a risk taken for someone else isn't always a bad investment."

Elia turned the cup in her hands. "I didn't think I believed anything," she said, low. "Not until I heard her voice."

Zane's gaze lifted. "You know who it is," he said. Not accusatory. A hand extended across a gap in the dark.

Elia's throat closed. She didn't answer. She was suddenly twelve again, sitting on a kitchen counter while her mother peeled an orange into a single spiral, whispering words the Union had taken out of mouths—rebellion, defiance, democracy, soul. Her mother's back to the door, Band white, hair braided. *Everything you need is hidden in the spine of the red book.*

The voice on the tape wasn't only familiar. It knew what to do with Elia's bones.

Zane didn't press. He turned the empty cup between his hands, then set it aside. "We've heard fragments," he said. "Partial broadcasts. Hisses that claim they were once words. But yours—" He stopped. "That might be the only clean piece left."

Mireya filled the doorway as if the room had been built for her silhouette. She held a small machine like a relic: an old-world player with guts replaced by scavenged loyalty, its speakers rebuilt and sanded smooth.

"Let's hear it," she said.

Elia's hand hovered over her pocket, then plunged. The cassette's plastic knocked her knuckles. The crooked ink—REMEMBER AMERICA—looked more crooked than yesterday, as if the letters had shifted to keep up with her pulse. She passed the tape to Mireya.

The room's hum pulled tight. Kade slid into the jamb. A woman still wearing a half-untied apron slipped in behind him. Somewhere close by a kettle began to rattle; someone hushed it with a towel. The world outside the door shrank to the size of the player's narrow mouth.

Mireya seated the cassette with a reverence she did not give people. The machine whirred. The speakers breathed once, twice—static, sand rubbing itself raw—and then the voice arrived.

If you're hearing this, they didn't wipe it all. They'll try. But memory isn't stored in systems. It lives in us.

They can take your freedom. But they can't take what you remember. So, say it with me. Say it out loud. Remember America.

No one moved. No one exhaled. For a handful of heartbeats the station became a lung that had forgotten how to function.

Elia's skin prickled. The words went in the way a needle slides into a vein and keeps going—past body, into a place with no approved name.

Mireya's eyes closed, then opened. She nodded once, as if confirming a diagnosis she had been pretending not to suspect.

"It's her," she said. "It's the source."

A sound escaped at the doorway—half laugh, half sob— slapped back to silence by a palm before it could grow. The woman with the apron steadied herself on the frame as if the room had tilted.

Zane didn't look at anyone but Elia. "You just became the most important person in the underground," he said, quiet enough that only the room could hear.

She didn't feel important. She felt two floors might open and she would be asked to choose which to fall through.

Mireya ejected the tape and cradled it in both hands. "We do this properly," she said to the air. "We back it up a dozen ways. We analyze the metadata. We carry duplicates to places where the Grid can't breathe. We never play it twice in the same spot. We move before the model retrains."

A murmur of assent swept the doorway, rough and low. Someone outside called, "Lanterns down! Power to blue!" The station's lights softened a shade, sliding toward caution.

Kade stood with his hostility tucked away and his hunger naked. "If it's clean, it moves," he said.

Zane reached past Elia, brushing her wrist, and lifted the bowl to stack it with the others. He checked her face as a medic checks for concussion: pupils, color, presence. "You're steady?"

"No," Elia said truthfully. "But I'm here."

He accepted that with a half nod, which meant good enough to move.

The station shifted into a rhythm Elia could feel in the bones of the floor—people assigned to tasks with a sentence, materials moved with economy, a watch set with the flick of two fingers. A thin woman with a sparrow tattoo at her throat took the cassette from Mireya and vanished under the arch, flanked by two boys who looked born with knives and had decided to be kinder than their faces.

Mireya turned to Elia. "You need a place to lay your head for an hour," she said. "You won't sleep. No one sleeps the first night. You'll lie there and listen to all the noises the Union told you were dangerous. Then you'll start learning which ones matter."

Elia's mouth twitched. "You always talk that way?"

"Only when I mean it," Mireya said. "Come."

They moved through the station. People did not brush against Elia. They made space and then watched how she filled it. A man with a handmade prosthetic forearm tightened a screw with his teeth and winked as if to say: we are all artificers of one kind or another. A small girl who should have been asleep sat cross-legged on a pallet, whispering a song to a scrap doll with button eyes. The melody wormed into Elia's ear with that circular persistence children's songs own—the kind that predated algorithms and would outlive them.

Mireya opened a small space carved into the wall—a former utility closet, now honest about its size. A pallet. A rolled blanket. A crate with a jug and a tin cup. A hook with a shirt that might fit. The air smelled of oil and wool and human breath. The absence of a speaker in the ceiling felt like a dare.

"Door doesn't lock," Mireya said.

"That supposed to make me feel safe?" Elia asked.

"It's supposed to make you feel watched," Mireya said. "We don't have cameras. We have each other." She started to leave, then looked back. "You say it's real because you heard it. That's not proof. If that voice is what I think it is, we will test it ten ways from the middle until its truth could withstand a rainfall of acid."

"And if it can't?" Elia asked.

"Then you'll leave before I have to ask," Mireya said, and went.

Elia sat on the pallet. The blanket scratched her palms. Phantom vibrations tickled her wrist where the Band usually rested; her nervous system tried to stand on a floor that wasn't there and stumbled. She pressed her thumb into the place the band should have been until she felt her own pulse—fast and irregular and alive.

Someone passed the doorway and paused. Zane. He held out something wrapped in cloth: a square of dark bread, dense as a book.

"You look like someone forgot to feed you for a decade," he said.

"Close," she said, taking it. Their fingers brushed and both pretended not to notice. He leaned his shoulder to the frame like someone who knew what his body could lean on.

"You okay?" he asked again, softer.

"No."

"Good," he said. "Means you're not numb."

He turned the cloth once in his hands, as if searching for words in it. "Mireya's not wrong," he said finally. "We can't take anything on faith. That voice could be a Union plant designed to make us hope too loud."

"It isn't," Elia said, and if there was one thing she was sure of tonight, it was that.

His mouth tipped. "I believe you," he said. "Doesn't mean I can act like it yet."

"How do you decide when to act?"

"When doing nothing feels like lying," he said. "You should get some rest."

She let her eyes close for one breath. The room slid.

A desk. A lamp. An old recorder waits on scarred wood, red light steady. A woman sits, braid tight, shoulders squared. Elia's chest says mother; the face won't land.

A man stands in the doorway, tall and lean, a scar through one brow. He doesn't enter. "Don't do this. Don't leave me."

The woman's hand covers the recorder. Elia reaches past—click. The sound prints into bone. The man catches her wrist, warm and rough, thumb to eyebrow—tap, tap, tap.

"Left side. Three-count. Find me even if they change our names."

She hears her own voice answer: "I promise." White flares. Lemon antiseptic floods the air. Hands remove and label. The vow tears into static and hides.

Elia's eyes opened to stone and wool and breath. The rhythm still ticked in her wrist.

Kade stood with his arms folded, trying less to look older and more to be useful. "Mireya wants you both," he said. "Lab."

"Coming," Zane said. He glanced at Elia. "You don't have to be there."

"Yes," Elia said. "I do."

The lab was a long counter bolted to the back of an old kiosk, its surface littered with the guts of machines—transistor guts laid out like organs, wires braided and labeled, a pair of magnifying lenses clipped to a lamp like eyes on stalks. The sparrow-throated woman had the cassette opened as carefully as a surgeon opens a chest. She did not handle it gently; she handled it with knowledge of what hurt and what would not.

"It's tape, not myth," she said without looking up. "Fiber base, magnetic coating. Edges worn here and here. Roller abrasion consistent with use but not overuse. Splice?" She pried a corner and shook her head. "No. Original runtime intact."

Mireya hovered, not because she doubted the work but because she respected it.

"Metadata," Zane said.

The woman snorted. "From a cassette?"

"Carrier residues. Environmental noise. Harmonic fingerprints from whatever room recorded it," he said. "You know how to make air talk."

She flicked him a glance that meant: fine. She fed the tape into a device with four manufacturer marks and a sister's name scratched on the side. The machine chirred and drew a profile—peaks and valleys like a mountain range.

"Hum at sixty Hertz," she said. "Power grid from before Union standardization. That's good." She zoomed into a thin band of hiss. "Birds."

Elia leaned in. "Birds?"

"In the pause between words. You can't hear them, but they're there. City birds. Not the Union's sonic-scarers. Pigeons or starlings. Old street that still had sky." She tapped another point. "And this? A door hinge whining. Metal on metal. Older stock."

Mireya's eyes flicked to Elia's face, measuring the tremor that started in her jaw and chose not to stop. "You want to say something," Mireya said.

"Elia," Zane warned.

"It's my mother," Elia said. The sentence ripped itself free like a hooked fish. "That's my mother's voice."

No one spoke. The station seemed to take a step back to give the words room.

Mireya didn't flinch. "We'll prove it," she said, which was mercy and also law. "Do you have other recordings? Anything with her voice?"

"No," Elia said. "Nothing survived." She saw her apartment the day after the soft purge, every trace of her mother sanitized into situation normal.

Zane's hand brushed her elbow once. Quick enough to deny. Solid enough for skin to remember.

"Even without the match," the sparrow-throated woman said, tapping the waveform, "this is clean. Not a Union fake. Their filters leave fingerprints. This doesn't."

Mireya's shoulders lowered a notch. "So," she said, thinking aloud, "we make twelve copies onto different carriers—tape, crystal, printed code. We spread them across stations. We build triggers so if one goes dark, the others scatter. We plan an uplink to bounce a thirty-second segment through an obsolete satellite and hijack the Broadcast for a breath."

"You hijack the Broadcast and Carrow comes through the ground," Zane said.

"Carrow comes anyway," Mireya said. "I prefer choosing when."

Kade, slate in hand, kept his voice even. "Department response dips for one cycle post-breach. Exploit the trough. Change pattern after every success."

"Which is exactly why they'll expect it," Zane said without heat. "They read the same stories we do."

Elia listened as if her body had emptied and the room had poured in. *Mother* lay coiled low—heavy and hot and changing shape. In the city, *mother* was a designation on a chart. Here it was a voice that had learned to dodge erasure and teach others to dodge it too.

A bell clinked somewhere in the station—three notes, close together. Conversation thinned.

Mireya's head turned. "Perimeter check," she said. Her voice wasn't afraid. It wasn't calm. It was ready.

A runner skidded into the doorway, breathless, sweat pinning hair to his forehead. He didn't look at Elia. He looked at Mireya as if the floor had become a cliff.

Before he could speak, Mireya cut a glance at Elia and stepped close enough that Elia could see the tiny scar at the corner of her mouth, the one you earn biting your own face to keep from saying a thing.

"If you're lying, girl," she said, voice flat as a knife's side, "you won't leave this station alive."

Zane leaned to Elia's ear, his words a low braille only she could read. "You realize they'll kill us both before they let that tape slip away."

The runner found his breath. His voice tore like cloth. "Union drones—they've found us."

CHAPTER 8
THE BANNED BOOKS

Sirens bit down. Blue washed the station. Lanterns slid to caution.

"Split and scatter," Mireya said. "Master east. Decoys north and south. Library team with me."

The sparrow-throated tech slid in; cassette wrapped in cloth. She pressed it into Elia's palm. "Master rides with the finder."

Elia shoved it into her pocket.

"On my left," Zane said, tapping her wrist. "Count three."

A runner cut past. "Drones in the west vents!"

"Move," Mireya snapped. "To the archive."

They crossed the chamber's ribs at a slant. Blue threw hard shadows. People flowed without colliding. Knives vanished. Paper moved hand to hand. A child slept through it with a doll under her chin.

Zane angled them toward a pillar painted with a laughing eye. His palm touched stone three quick times. A seam breathed. Damp air kissed skin. A panel slid. He wedged a thread of cloth to stop a squeal.

"Hidden stacks first," Zane said. "Two minutes."

They slipped into a narrow throat ribbed with shelves that never made any map. Dust carried the low musk of cloth handled too many times. No Broadcast. No tags. Only outlawed paper.

"Elia," Zane murmured.

"Red book," she answered. Her mother's voice walked up her spine.

Everything you need is hidden in the spine of the red book.

"Colors everywhere," he said. "Which red?"

"Not a title. The spine."

Her hands moved—top shelf, middle, bottom. Red, then red, then another red. Too clean. Too new. She pushed deeper where spines had chipped down to cardboard. One leaned wrong, wider at the back than the front. Cloth buckled along the seam.

"This one."

"Work fast."

She eased it out. No title. No author. Weight off by a hair. A thin cut ran the glue line. Someone had slit it and set the cloth back.

A pick slid down the gutter. The cloth sighed. The spine opened. Inside—a cavity no thicker than a fingernail. A clear shard nested there, thin as a match, wrapped with a strip of folded paper.

She breathed once through her nose, pinched both pieces free, and sealed the cloth again.

Dust drifted at the far end. Zane's palm lifted. Stop.

An orb nosed in, lens slit drinking air. A hair-thin beam combed the shelf edge, then hung, undecided.

He slid a spike into his fingers and waited for the pivot. Snap. White flared. The shell twitched and sagged to the floor, plastic smoking, a pinched whine dying under the shelves.

A second orb peered to the gap. Wrong angle, no shot. It read the drop in heat and sent the change away.

"Partial ping," Zane said, voice flat. "Our door's watched now."

"Kade," Elia whispered.

He ghosted in from the cross-aisle with a coil at his hip and a slate under his arm. "Model's reweighting off the last breach," he said. "Heat plus movement plus clustering. Don't bunch."

"Routes," Zane said.

"Valve Row buys you quiet," Kade answered. "Conduit Three is fast and watched."

Zane nodded. His jaw clicked once when Kade stepped close, gone as fast as it came. "Quiet. We cut through stacks."

Crystal under her shirt; paper strips into her pocket beside the cassette. The weight sat true. Not heavy. Important.

They backed out between shelves. Zane pulled the panel to a thumb's width and let it breathe shut on the cloth wedge.

Coins on a wire gave a dull ring at his touch. Clear.

"Step on the bolts," he said. "Not the plates."

"On your left," she answered. "Counting."

"In. Hold. Three. Out."

The vent coughed. Air pushed. Dust jumped. Zane tapped her wrist on three and slid them under the burst. They cut right, shoulders narrow, weight quiet. A beam scratched past an opening and missed. He never moved straight—always off the model's favorite path.

Kade held up a shallow dish wired at the back. "I can buy twenty seconds," he said. "Old test tone. Confuses the model's ear. You owe me a coil."

"You keep a ledger?" Zane asked.

"Sector 9 trained me to count," Kade said, mouth curving once, gone. "I use it for us now." He set the dish on a valve wheel. "Go."

Valve Row turned slick where a seam wept. Zane steered Elia along grit in the aggregate. His hand found her sleeve for one stride, then let go. A ladder's slot opened to a grate; his fingers read the seam and left it closed.

"Watched," he said.

"Conduit Twelve is blind two doors down," Kade added. "Smells worse. Safer."

"Smells worse?" Elia said.

"Coolant bled last year. The model avoids it."

They took Twelve. Air burned the back of the throat for three steps, then steadied. Plates lined the floor, bolts dark at the corners.

"Toe. Heel. Stud to stud," Zane said.

She matched him through the run. The cassette knocked her hip once, a small reminder. The crystal warmed against skin. She let the count sit under her ribs and drove oxygen where it needed to go.

"Dead bulb ahead," Zane said when the hall pinched. "Read fast."

A utility bite opened—one meter by one. A bulb burned above a broken switch. No sensor winked on its cap. Zane cupped his hand and unfolded the paper strip with a careful roll.

Straight strokes, no wasted loops. Five words:
To speak, use memory's bones.

Under the line, three taps drawn in a row. An arrow to the left margin.

Skin at her eyebrow prickled where a thumb had once pressed tap, tap, tap.

"That's her," Elia said.

"We prove it," Zane answered. He refolded the strip and placed it back in her hand. His thumb almost skimmed her knuckle, then he thought better of it. "Keep both on you."

Soft soles brushed stone two corridors over. Two sets. Kade cocked his head.

"My decoy ran out," he said. "We go."

They threaded the valves, timed the hum, let air wrap their heat, and angled through a service run until the blue wash thinned and the stone pulled close.

Mireya waited at a rusted doorway blotched with mineral bloom. Fire jars burned low along the approach. Heat, glue, old smoke. Stone held a slow breath.

Her palm pressed a scabbed rectangle of plastic. A single green vein woke. The seal let go with a tired hiss.

The archive opened—a wound.

Blue thinned to gray in the tunnels. Kade's ping: *perimeter stable; drones drifting west on a false trail.* Mireya nodded once—a window to breathe.

Rows of whale-boned metal laced with wire and faith. Crates stamped by dead shipping firms. Books stacked, layered, leaning, arguing in spines and titles. No grid. No obedient shelves. Intentional disorder that refused the Union's order.

The Diary of Anne Frank. 1984. A People's History of the United States. The Federalist Papers. Sula. Fahrenheit 451. Letters from Birmingham Jail. The Constitution. The Declaration of Independence. The Bill of Rights. Songbooks with mended spines. Chapbooks. Comics with bright covers scarred white by scraping. Cookbooks with pencil notes that turn measures into memory. Children's stories rounded by small thumbs. *The Velveteen Rabbit* sat on a crate, spine hand-stitched in thread that didn't match and therefore told the truth.

Strips of old sun clung inside frames propped on crates—windows to weather that never reached this deep.

Elia stepped in and kept her heels soft. The floor felt consecrated. Dust turned in slow currents. Words pressed from every direction without a speaker telling her what to feel.

A crate marked in marker: *CIVIL RIGHTS — 1950–2050.* Ink feathered along fibers. A thin book lifted under her fingers. Grain met her—images that burned and froze in the same breath. Marchers. Faces. Hand-cut signs the Union would have flagged as destabilizing before erasure. *NO JUSTICE, NO PEACE. BLACK LIVES MATTER. WE THE PEOPLE MEANS ALL OF US.* A man in a chair framed by a crowd. A woman in a hijab holding a flag with a grip that set the fabric stern. Children locking arms in front of vehicles built to excuse harm.

The charge in the photographs had no sanctioned word. Not anger. Not grief. Truth.

"What did they call this?" Elia asked, voice low.

"Nostalgia risk. Emotional dissonance. Cultural contamination," Mireya said. Smoke roughened the words. No drama. Diagnosis.

"It's history."

"Not under them." She moved to a metal cabinet, paint flaking in curls, and unlatched the door. Bands lay coiled in neat rows, every one scoured where teeth had bitten. "Everyone here removed theirs," she said. "Some of us the hard way."

A pale crescent crossed the thin skin of her wrist. No need to ask. The scar answered.

Elia's own wrist felt light, tender. Phantom pressure prickled along the bone where the Band had sat for years. She stopped rubbing the skin.

Mireya reached past the Bands and drew out a plain journal, corners softened. No cover title. Inside flap: a name pressed so hard the page held the shadow where the nib bit—*INEZ WARD*.

"My mother," Elia said.

"We've had it for years," Mireya said. "Pulled from a resistance drop in Sector 12 after a purge. Logged as decoy. The tape told us what it is."

No apology. Only survival math, false fronts and hidden cores.

Elia opened the book. The hand matched the cassette's label, letters leaning into wind. Words hurried and sure:

They won't win by killing us. They'll win by making our children forget we existed. America wasn't perfect. That's what made it worth fighting for. Don't worship the past. Learn from it. Then scream its truth into the next generation.

Heat rose through paper where pressure had gone down years ago. Throat tightened. Pages turned under greedy fingers. Ink blurred before she knew tears had formed. Paper bruised under her grip.

Silence stood with her until breath steadied. Mireya's face burned and held at once.

"My father stacked his books in the yard the night the Grid went white," Mireya said. "History. Languages. Smuggled fragments. He burned them before the Union reached our block. Said better ash than their silence. I called him a coward. Twelve. Thought I'd live forever. By morning, half the building had vanished without smoke. My brother hummed through the purge. One held note to keep the walls from forgetting. Thirteen. He asked if the air smelled sweet. It did. I never heard his voice again. So, we keep this place. If we don't, they get to be right about us."

The story left only the straightness of her spine.

Elia pressed the journal to her sternum until bone met board. Old words moved through her and set her frame. She wandered the stacks with the journal warm against her ribs. Fingers lifted dust from titles. *The Constitution* surprised her—a country's hinge in the weight of a small bird. Fragile. Burnable. Pocketable. Drones could mark a yard's fire and register compliance. The Union did not fear crowds. They feared memory. Memory made questions, and questions pried at doorframes.

Paper and glue and stone filled her lungs. Breath found a rhythm without software. A hairline in her life widened— no pain, only fact.

She took the journal to her pallet. No one stopped her. Zane passed the corridor with grease to the wrist and a coil on his shoulder. He tipped his chin—a quiet *you found it* that hit hard.

Letters turned to gray bands and snapped back when she blinked. The stove burned to copper, then to a seam of dull coin. The station breathed in a key the city never taught.

Sleep came late and brought words that felt both known and new—*Freedom. Choice. Liberty.* On the tongue they rounded and warmed. In her chest they sparked.

Embers painted bars along curved steel when she woke. Silence left room for thought to pace. She flipped to the back. The hand loosened in the later entries—tails wider, pressure uneven, a walker's scrawl, a carrier who refused to set anything down:

They'll turn you against yourself first. You won't notice. One day you forget a song. Or your father's voice. Or how wind sounded before filters. If this survives, don't look for me. I'm not the answer. I remembered the question.

No goodbye. The last page had torn clean out. Fibers still looked fresh, as if the tears persisted.

Bare feet padded in. Mireya set down two mugs that steamed roasted grain. Elia had opened a picture book— watercolor bears refusing sleep because they feared missing the world. The brew tasted bitter and right. Pages turned. The room proved itself by working.

"You, okay?" Mireya asked at last.

"No," Elia said.

"That's the point."

A thin volume slid from a shelf into Mireya's hand. *Where the Sidewalk Ends.* She passed it across. A short poem shoved against order until laughter jumped from Elia's chest, sharp and single. No ceiling speaker pinged a warning. Bare wrist tingled with relief.

"They always watched," Mireya said. "Now they adjust. Soft nudges until you forget your edge. They don't erase history. They replace it with compliance."

Two fingers tapped her temple. Her gaze slid past Elia, past shelves, toward a night only she could see.

"The night my city went white, the air turned candy sweet. Mothers pressed hands over mouths and called it a game. The mist fell. You could pretend it was weather. I learned silence can pound. Music carries memory. Memory makes us dangerous."

Zane found Elia in a booth of crates and blankets. Photographs circled her—strangers laughing, faces mid-chant behind cardboard words, a woman standing on a police car with her hair in motion.

"You're nesting," he said, filling the jamb without drawing a lens.

"I'm cataloging," she said. "They cataloged us to erase us. I'm building an index they can't read."

He crouched with a sure fold. A page came out of his jacket, creased to the size of a mouth.

"Belongs with your journal," he said. "Ration bin near Sector 6. I didn't know what it was then."

Water had blurred an edge. The letters belonged to her mother. Pressure lived in the page more than ink.

They'll come for the voices first. When they do, don't go quiet. Scream louder. Until your voice becomes someone else's memory. Remember America.

The plaza lifted around her—the statue's round absence, panels scrolling lullabies, children reciting cadence while a second rhythm ran under it. A lift mirror holding a neutral face built for safe passage. The mask named itself and slid off.

"I want to help," she said.

"You are," Zane answered on reflex.

She had already kept the cassette alive and run where no module taught running.

"Really help," she said. "Fragments, hiding, reacting—it isn't enough."

Mireya's shadow arrived first, then her body. Arms crossed. Kindness armed.

"You've got a plan," Mireya said.

"I worked at Equilibrium," Elia said. "I know the linguistic filters. Suppression by frame. They bury words in code and tell you code is the only language that matters. They shift weight until a syllable can't stand. I know the seams. I stitched a few."

"How?" Zane said. Not doubt—engineering.

"With this." She raised the journal, then tapped her temple. "And this."

Mireya's eyes flicked to Zane and back, a circuit closing.

"You want a virus?" Zane said.

"No." Elia shook her head. "They expect viruses. I want a memory. Salt their language with words that won't dissolve. Hide a line so deep in their filters the filters carry it, pass it, protect it, because they accept it as self. No pirate banners. No blaze that dies. A seed. A lullaby folded into their sleep."

"Explain memory," Mireya said.

"Equilibrium runs semantic weightings—matrices assigning risk to terms and pairs. They downshift protest, strike, uprising until those words fog. They boost harmony, stability, and calm. But the matrix is language. We can tune it the other way. We don't hammer. We sing. We teach it to recognize a phrase they forgot to scrub because they didn't know where it lived. Embed the line across low-risk paths—children's content, counseling scripts, nutrition guides. Places their heuristics nap. Whisper the same line into a thousand small places until it becomes baseline."

Elia set the folded strip on the table. "We use my mother's words," she said. "They travel."

Zane's face eased to a degree, the amount a lock gives when a pick finds the ward. "You'll need entries."

"Three," she said. "Maintenance. Counsel. Dietary. Maintenance because no one reads machine chatter unless something screams. Counsel because scripts flex and already fake empathy—we hide real empathy there. Diet because everyone eats and no one suspects a ration pack of teaching revolt."

"They'll catch the first," Mireya said. "They always do if it works."

"Then the second reads as correction," Elia said. "The third stays buried until the first two route."

"We don't fight where they're strong," she added. "We fight where they're lazy."

Mireya stepped close. Stitches along her jacket cuff had been set for endurance, not show.

"Once you start, you don't get to step back," she said. "You put your voice against theirs, they come. Not to erase. To repurpose. They turn us into lessons."

"I know," Elia said. The knowledge felt less brave than gravity.

"Good." Mireya nodded to Zane. "If we do it, the relay carries it."

"We harden the mesh," Zane said. "Split the path. Paint one route bright so they chase and never smell the other." He studied Elia the way he studied doors—counting hinges, checking swell. "You'll need unfiltered corpora. Old language bodies. We have some. Enough to map gaps. But we'll need a fresh Equilibrium update. Weights shift every cycle."

He spoke like a man who reads wind.

Knuckles tapped a shelf. Somewhere, a drawer slid open. The station's lattice answered a human rhythm it had learned.

"We don't plan hungry," Mireya said. "Eat. Work while we talk. Then map routes. That order keeps us alive."

They ate lentils with garlic and time—the kind of time only a safe room affords. The station shifted into intention. A battery took a gentler pitch so the hum wouldn't drown a code word. Two teens braided copper harnesses and argued in low voices about rhyme versus rhythm for memory travel. An old woman who had taught in a city that denied its schools existed taught a child to read from a grocery flyer, sounding letters and ignoring pictures.

Zane vanished and returned with hands black to the wrist. He handed Elia a cloth without remark. Fingers touched. Work swallowed the touch.

He hooked two fingers at Elia and Mireya. In the lab corner, the sparrow-throated tech had opened machine bellies and sorted organs into bowls marked in grease pencil—a survival taxonomy.

"We need an old Harmonizer," Zane said. "Pre-consolidation. Compression left artifacts you can braid. They dumped them because the artifacts smelled human."

"You know artifacts?" he asked Elia.

"A ghost caught in sound," she said.

He nodded. With the tech he pieced a pried-open interface from parts meant for other arguments and taught them to cooperate. His mouth flattened at a bad solder— someone had run before tin cooled. He smoothed it and made it hold.

"Where did you get the page?" she asked, tuning an oscillator until the whine fell from irritant to thread.

"Sector 6," he said. "Ration center scheduled for demolition. They saw wrappers and a calendar and stopped. I look where people stop." He slid a hand into his boot, palmed his insole, and showed a clear shard etched with a single line. *Truth doesn't die. It waits.* He didn't need to say it. The words hummed through steel.

"Why trust me?" she asked.

"I don't," he said. "Not yet. I'm not asking for trust. I'm asking you to keep choosing what you chose when you stood up in that room."

"What if I choose wrong?"

"Then we pay," he said. "Loud."

By the time the Harmonizer purred, and a cracked tablet lit with a relay map—thin veins over the city's dead graph—the room had slipped toward night though no window marked it. Voices dropped out of habit. The day folded small to fit through.

Elia read a paragraph from the journal into the circuit to hear how metal answered. Syllables came back thinned, smoothed. Her finger found a dip in the return.

"There," she said. "Filter weight. Feed it with harmless content—their calm—and our line can ride under."

"We'll choose the right line," Mireya said.

Kade stood in the doorway, hunger tucked away. "What if the right line is a name?" he asked. "What if the first word they can't smooth is a person?"

"Then we keep that person breathing long enough to deserve it," Mireya said.

His jaw set and stayed shut.

Elia spread her palm on the torn last page and felt the absence press back. The plaza. The statue. Children at cadence. A woman mouthing *LIBERTY* as sacrament. Carrow's Even Diction. Drone beams moving through trees. Zane's mother's hand on his cheek. Mireya's father's books stacked in a yard. A boy's held note. Honey-sweet fog. A shard against a pulse until warmth proved it. Words as seeds. Code as soil.

She laid the folded strip beside the map. "Start with this," she said, voice low, steady. "To speak, use memory's bones."

A breath. "I want a line they can't hear without feeling. A line that turns every Band into a liar. They'll mark it calm and carry it into every apartment, then wake at midnight because a word knocks inside their ribs and won't let them sleep."

Her voice didn't rise. It deepened.

"I want to make them remember."

CHAPTER 9
CODE: LIBERTY

No-echo sweep," Mireya said.

Her voice ran the length of the station and came back balanced. Lanterns slid to caution. The hum of the lattice dipped, then steadied. Doors breathed shut. Talk fell from sentence to signal.

"Vault custody," she added. "Master goes under glass. Two signatures."

The sparrow-throated tech stepped to Elia, palms visible, a strip of white cloth in one hand. "Pocket," she said.

Elia drew the cassette and set it in the cloth. The tech wrapped it tight, then held it up to the lantern for one heartbeat so the grease-pencil code on the knot could set. "Finder?" she asked.

"Here," Mireya said. "And me."

They touched their thumbs to the cloth knot. The knot drank the print and flashed once. The tech vanished with the bundle under the arch toward the vault, one room down, mesh door, two locks that folded back to the wall when they were pleased.

"Runner staging?" Mireya asked.

"Joren has the eggs," Zane answered. "Pouch across chest. Half charge each."

Kade's voice cut in from the lowline, steady as a metronome. "Outer scan bands warming. Scrapers on the west side. Nothing inside the circle yet. If that changes, you'll taste it first."

"Copy," Mireya said. "Zane, with Elia. Lab."

The corridor to the lab kept its ceiling low so sound would not travel. When the door shut, the room pulled in around them. Wires fell in skeins. Every surface had been repurposed twice and was not through being repurposed. An old pediatric core sat on a cart; its shell painted with cartoon whales that had outlived the children they were meant to soothe. Three Harmony home consoles blinked the soft blue they had been taught. Their guts now listened.

Elia slid her hands under the cracked keyboard. The old plastic was smooth and warm from other hands, other nights. The screen lifted a grid. She tapped her forefinger once, twice, three times on the table's edge and the rhythm settled her spine.

"Say it for me," Zane said, standing back a step, posture loose, ready.

"The plan?" she asked.

"The word."

She breathed. "Remember."

He nodded once. "Count on my mark."

His wrist touched her. One, two, three. Her hands moved.

She pulled the maintenance channel up first, the low chatter machines mutter to each other when no one is supposed to be listening. Then she opened the counsel prompts where empathy lives on rails. Then checkout totals where digits grind. Each carried a thin carrier band no one respected, a useful forgetfulness born of victory. She spun a courier into the weave, not a message, a pulse. The pulse matched their rhythm and borrowed the city's.

Code compiled. The fan's pitch lifted and held. The screen threw a curve of approvals. She watched the curve and felt her body dip with it.

A blink. The curve steadied. Her eyes closed without consent.

Heat. A room with a desk. A mic propped on two books. Static feeding back against the window. Her own face in a dark screen that held her reflection in shards. Not her mother. Her mouth. The way she formed certain consonants as if they wanted to escape and had to be coaxed back.

"Don't," a man said behind her.

His hands rested on her shoulders, warm, certain. One thumb climbed to her brow, pressed once, twice, three. The scar under the brow moved with it.

"If I don't, we vanish," she said.

"Not this way."

"It is the way we have."

She looked at the mic. She put her mouth near and whispered the words that still lived on the strip she had found in a red spine. "To speak, use memory's bones."

"Don't leave me," he said.

His voice carried the rattle of a man who had run too many stairs. She saw only his hands but knew the rest. A jaw set when carrying weight. A mouth that quirked when a plan worked.

She pressed record.

She woke with a breath she did not trust. Her hand had lifted to her brow. Her fingers were on the old scar before she knew she had moved.

Zane had not touched her. He had braced a palm on the console to keep it from rattling so the fan's pitch would not climb into alarm. He watched her from the angle that let him see the doorway, the screen, her face.

"You dropped for ten seconds," he said. "Install compiled."

"I saw—" She stopped. A lie would be worse than silence. "I saw a desk. A recording. A hand on my brow."

He did not ask whose hand. He moved the chair closer to the table so her knees would clear when she leaned in. "Give your hands something to do," he said. "They shake less that way."

She breathed into count. "In. Hold. Three. Out." The shake steadied.

"Tell me the shape of it," he said, meaning the code.

She named the channels. She did not call them by the Union's names. She said what they were. The places where language rides sound and sound rides unexamined paths.

"We fracture across frequency," she said. "We bury the line inside carrier bands where their heuristics sleep. One name for it only. Frequency-fracture. Then we put a mask over meaning so the screeners see calm and let it pass. Semantic masking. I won't repeat it again."

"Good," Zane said. "No chant for them to hear."

She threaded the new stream into the maintenance hum. The courier shook once as if testing a leg and then stood under its new weight. She shaved edge from the obvious words and paired them to the Union's pillows so the scan would read soft while the ear heard metal. Remember with restore. Memory with structure. Freedom with shape.

"Don't double-tap a node," Zane said. "We bounce across sectors. Education loop. Grocery scripts. Counsel. Meditation. If one raises a flag, the others keep moving."

"I skew to off-peak," she answered. "Fewer eyes. The machine will assume noise."

"Noise that teaches."

She built the pulse against the Broadcast's metronome. She did not write sentences. She set a beat a body would adopt if it heard it enough times. Under the beat she buried the old line in pieces thin as hair. M-E-M riding M-E-D-I. The R of remember hiding behind the R of restore. A-M-E-R-I-C-A ghosting under numbers where a checkout total reads and does not think.

Kade's voice touched the lowline, matter of fact. "Reweighting on the outer scan lanes. Scrapers sniffing along the west vent stack. Nothing on the inner rings. You have space if you keep your angles strange."

"Copy," Zane said. He pointed to the decoy console. "I'll throw something bright into a watched lane when you send the real. They'll pounce on red. You'll ride under yellow."

"When you throw bright," Elia said, "you don't run alone."

His mouth tipped at the edge. "Worried?"

"Effective," she said. "Stay on my left."

"Count three," he said. It was not a joke.

"Count three," she repeated, and the corners of his mouth eased the fraction that stands in for a smile when the room is full of machines that would rat you out for joy.

Three hours thinned to threads. The station moved above them in a low, constant music, soft talk, a pan lid tapped to signal safe, a generator that meant to keep faith. Mireya stood in the lab doorway for one minute and placed her palm on the whale sticker's shell. She listened with her hand.

"You're at the gate?" she asked.

"Courier is loaded," Elia said. "One tap and it breathes."

"Vault is sealed," Mireya said. "Two signatures and a dead switch on the hinge. If they kick the door, they hit an empty hole. Kade?"

"Outer ring is not closing yet," he said. "Scan traffic is heavier than an hour ago. Their scrapers move in pairs. No heat."

Mireya's eyes went to Elia's fingers. A split had opened along her thumb where a wire had bit earlier. A smear of ink darkened her ring finger, the journal's residue. Mireya turned her wrist and showed her own pale crescent scar under the lantern. "We do this clean," she said. "No flinch. No partials. If we hurt, we make it worth it."

"Understood," Elia said.

Mireya left her with the quiet the room saved for work. Zane crouched alongside the bench on the balls of his feet, the way a man sits when he intends to move fast the moment his body agrees. "She tells it straight," he said, eyes on the screen. "She doesn't tell you how she woke three times that first night and held her breath because drones ran heat in the hall. She built four walls so she could argue back. That's the whole story."

"And yours?" Elia asked before she could convince herself not to.

He rolled a shoulder. "I passed. I learned the Broadcast cadence and said what they wanted in the tone they preferred. I carried a shard in my shoe and remembered not to limp. I ran messages for three years before Mireya agreed to stand in a room with me without glass."

He ran his thumb along the console's edge, straightening a peel of old tape. "First time I heard a child laugh again, I thought it was a drone. Took a month to stop thinking it sounded wrong."

That was the place in the story where another person would touch a wrist or a jaw and make a moment soft. She did not. She turned to the screen and gave her hands more to do. She wrote a handshake for the courier that limped on purpose so the scan would read wear, not threat.

Night braided itself through the station. The archive under their feet breathed heat to the bones. Elia took her mother's journal to a circle of lamplight. She read until the words thinned, lost edges, and swam back to clarity when she blinked them into place again. She did not hunt for new lines. She kept the cadence in her mouth. One sentence rose above the others and stayed:

They will call you dangerous before they call you true.

"You steady?" Zane asked from the doorway. The word steady in his mouth meant present, not calm.

"No," she said. "I don't want to be."

"Good," he said.

He slid down the wall and sat beside her with a grace he must have practiced when rooms were smaller than his body. He lifted the battered reader he had tuned to the lattice's gait.

"Beta nodes are answering. Three phrases hit. Two flagged and quarantined. One went through."

"What line?" she asked.

"Let us not forget the shape of freedom, even if its name is dust. Night counsel. Two districts."

She shut her eyes. Somewhere a counseling script had spoken the word freedom, and a child had heard it without a siren's teeth closing on her bones. The world did not crack. Hairlines found each other.

"What happens when they notice?" she asked.

"They will," he said. "Sooner if we are good."

"And then?"

"They shut doors. They sweeten air. They call it safety. They hunt." He looked at her, the part that was not gentle and not cruelty meeting her eye. "Or this moves faster than they do."

She leaned her head back into wood. "Do you think people want the memory. Or do they just want the noise to stop."

"Wanting the noise to stop is a memory," he said after a breath. "Bones remembering that peace was earned once, not issued."

At 03:00 the station pinged, a ring thin and exact. The lowline carried Mireya's voice stripped of decoration. "Sector Four confirms delivery. Passive index reached. No flag. No resistance."

The temperature shifted. Someone somewhere tried not to laugh and failed on the breath out. Boots scraped quick and quiet. Zane stood in the lamp's circle and handed Elia a thermal slip, cheap paper that curled when you breathed on it. "Uncensored," he said. "Morning cadence in two districts."

They can take your name. They can take your family. But they can't take what you carry in your memory. Remember America.

Words that felt too thin for the weight they would make in rooms not built for truth. Somewhere a child asked, "What does America mean?" and for six seconds a mother did not know which lie to choose and considered telling the truth.

Mireya filled the doorway with jacket half zipped and hair shoved back by a hand that had moved fast.

"We stirred the water," she said. "Two cells are dark. Eleven and the Belt's edge. No heat where they were. Either they left before the net dropped or they didn't get away." No drama. Math. "We keep seeding fragments or we burn the whole voice. We have minutes, not hours."

Zane shook his head. "Full drop dies in ten seconds. We lose the lane and anyone who holds it open."

"They adapt," Mireya said. "They always adapt." Her gaze found Elia and rested there.

"I can fracture the voice," Elia said.

She did not have to search for the sentence. She had been building it between keystrokes.

"Not into parts. Into frequencies. They train their scans on content. We ride structure. We hide her cadence in carrier bands they left dirty when they standardized. Maintenance pings. Counsel empathy. Checkout totals. We do not send a line. We seed a thousand crumbs and let the lattice rebuild it at the far end."

Zane rubbed his jaw, the picture in his head turning three ways and failing twice. "You'll need unfiltered speech to shape the masks."

"We have enough to find the gaps," Elia said. "Their weights haven't changed in years. They won. They stopped listening."

Mireya did not nod. Elia felt the yes enter the room anyway. "Understand what happens when they trace the infection."

Elia slid the journal into the inside pocket she had sewn into her coat. Her wrist felt naked. The nakedness felt honest. "Then they will find someone who finally remembers."

"Runners to Blue," Mireya said into the lowline. "Echo team with me. Joren, wake the sleepers."

Joren arrived with his jacket crooked, and a transmitter pouch strapped across his chest. Wire ends showed where the canvas had been mended in a hurry by hands that meant the mending to last. He hovered at the threshold until Elia lifted a hand.

"My parents," he said. No preface. "Sector Three. They don't—" He swallowed. "They taught me to be quiet. Quiet kept us. If this reaches them, will they know."

"They will feel it," Elia said. "Even if the words aren't ready. Feeling is the first step."

The tendons in his neck loosened a fraction. He nodded and vanished into motion.

Zane moved through the lab touching small things that save lives later. He tightened a ground where the solder had lifted. He lowered the fan so the hum would not mask a low broadcast. He slid a square of foam under the pediatric core to quiet a rattle. He was not careful from fear. He was careful because time is a thing you can bank if you spend it right.

"Tell me the shard," Elia said while her fingers flew. She did not need it told. She wanted the air to hold it.

"She etched one line," he said. "Truth doesn't die. It waits." He lifted his insole and showed the sliver. Clear. Etching bright. "I read it under a blanket with the Band light turned to a lamp. I memorized the shape of the words in my mouth until sound wasn't necessary. When I ran, I lost everything heavy. The shard weighed nothing and kept me from floating away."

"You carried it until you didn't need to," she said.

"I still need it," he said. "Today I need you more."

She mapped the frequencies as rivers that run under rock and found the places where water always gets through. She planted stones to bend the current so the sound would arrive where it needed to and still claim coincidence. She taught empathy prompts to hold a poem in the corner of the mouth. She taught checkout totals to count a word among numbers. She braided meditation scripts with an off beat that would itch the ear until the mind supplied a missing name.

Echo techs checked coils. Joren looped a sling of hand-built transmitters under one arm, each egg packed in cloth. The low fire in the central grate burned blue to hide its smoke. Mireya moved from hand to hand with very little to say and everything to see. When she paused behind Elia, she touched the back of the chair with two fingers, the way you touch a hull before a launch. Not for luck. For witness.

The lowline cracked. "Zane," a voice said. Training held the panic down to neutral. "Outer spur is humming. New traffic on the scan band."

"How close," he asked.

"Close enough to matter."

He looked at Elia.

"We ride under it," she said. "Noise cover. They are shifting power. We take the layer they gave us."

"We also drown if we jump at the wrong second." He did not build a no into the sentence. He watched her hands.

"When I was little," Mireya said, settling a hip against the bench, eyes on the whale decal, "my brother would hum into a glass until we felt it in our teeth. When it hit, we knew it in the bone." She tilted her head. "Tell me when you feel it."

Elia felt it in her palms first, where nerves met plastic. The carrier band swelled, the way water warns of a fallen branch upstream without saying it. Maintenance traffic routed around a lockdown somewhere above them. She flipped the courier's handshake and set it to match a frequency the Union had forgotten mattered. "Now," she said.

Zane hit send. The pediatric core's light deepened from toy blue to bruise. The consoles blinked as if they meant to object, then remembered who they were before they were taught their manners. The courier moved. It moved the way a rumor moves when it happens to be true.

Joren's breath went out on a sound that could have been prayer. "Node A through," he said. "Echo backs. No flag. Node C—" His eyes narrowed. "Scraper sniffed. Moved on."

"Because we fed it the taste it expects," Elia said. "We keep it hungry in the wrong direction."

"Throwing bright," Zane said. He sent the decoy courier down a lane that would draw a scanner's eye. It shone. The scan pounced as if trained by the oldest of stories. The real courier slid by under the noise.

"Sector 4 confirms," the lowline said. "Sector 7 confirms. Eleven is dead. Belt is dead. Outer ring is static."

"Move before the seal tightens," Zane said.

"We move now," Mireya answered. "Joren, first leg. Kade, keep the scan in your teeth."

Kade's voice came back shaved down to essentials. "Reweighting," he said. "They tuned off content. They're sampling rhythm. Be ready to bend your metronome."

"I will," Elia said.

He paused. "Good."

Her hands shook once and were steady. She thought of the plaza and a woman's lips shaping *LIBERTY*. She thought of a boy's humming behind a door. She thought of her mother's lines and the shard's words and shelves of banned paper that had not ashed. She felt the new line settle inside the old line in her chest, a blade finding its sheath.

The lowline popped. "Outer ring is closing," Kade said. "Top of the hour. Sharp. You have a wedge if you stay strange."

"Echo team," Mireya said. "On my mark." She looked at Elia then, not asking for permission she did not need, counting whether the person in front of her was present enough to carry weight. Elia met the count.

"Then they will find someone who finally remembers," she said.

Zane braced one hand on the bench to stand. He hesitated a fraction of a second that holds the difference between caution and care. His fingers lifted toward her brow, stopped, and shifted to the strip on her thumb.

"Your wrap," he said. "You'll bleed on the keys."

"You'll throw your bright and get your jaw broken," she said.

He almost smiled. "Stay on my left."

"Count three," she said.

He tapped her wrist. One, two, three. The station moved.

Joren slid through the door with his pouch of eggs and a runner's breath in his chest. He passed the decoy route to his partner and took the dark one for himself. Mireya set her palm on the vault door as she went by, one beat for the names that had gone in under cloth, then lifted her hand and made no sign to any god.

They sent the second courier during a scan power shift. The third ran under a diagnostic ping. The fourth went through a counsel module that asked citizens to breathe and name one safe word. The fifth rode a grocery tally and hid in the zeroes. The sixth, seventh, eighth—small moves that bent riverbanks without drawing eyes.

Within an hour the lattice drank the seeds the way ground drinks rain after a drought. Kade called reweights that did not surprise him and closed circles that tried to outpace a body with a song under its ribs. The Union did not send a face. It sent pressure. Scrapers sniffed. Scanners pounced. The ring sealed. A lane opened when maintenance crew somewhere told a machine to quiet and forgot to tell the others what they had done.

"Again," Mireya said, every time Elia looked to her.

The pediatric core let slip a sound it had not made for a decade, a lullaby a metal mouth once gave to frightened children. Under the sugar of it, if you listened off the side of your ear, the phrase moved. Not spoken. Shaped.

Joren's voice dropped one register. "Sector 2," he said. "Night counsel returned a phrase. Full calm flag. No quarantine." He breathed. "They heard it."

"What did they hear?" Zane asked.

Joren read from the screen. "Remember the shape you were before you were told what to be."

It was not the whole line. It was enough.

The outer ring pulled tight, and the Belt stayed dead. Kade named three scanners working pairs, then a third with a noise profile he had not met before. "They are tuning to rhythm," he said. "They will catch a courier that breathes steady. Jag your metronome."

Elia shifted the heartbeat the courier rode. Off by half of a half count. The way a runner breathes when the body goes spare. The scan hesitated and went for the decoy instead.

Mireya's hand touched the back of Elia's chair again. Two fingers. Wood, then air. "We seed until the seal closes. Then we ghost."

"Copy," Zane said. He pointed to the route map where thin veins crossed old grid lines. "We have one more quiet channel along Valve Row." He glanced at Elia. "Your call."

She looked at the list of rooms the courier might touch—kitchens, therapy suites, lifts, counters where ration workers weighed carrots that had never seen sun. She thought of two cells that were dark and might be alive somewhere else. She thought of a single child in Sector 3 who had learned to sleep with a hand over her mouth because her father had told her games could save you.

"Send it," she said. "Then we go."

Joren ran. The pouch of eggs bumped his sternum. He did not trip. He did not look behind. The door swallowed him and gave no sound.

The courier slipped under a diagnostic beep and returned no flag. For fifteen breaths the room held the shape of a win. It did not smile. It did not cheer. It measured. And then the outer ring's tone changed in Kade's ear.

"Reweighting complete," Kade said. "They learned from us. They're scanning the breath. Ghost now."

Mireya lifted her hand. "Ghost."

Lanterns ate their own light. Zane slid the shard under his insole. Elia folded the strip and pressed her palm to her ribs where the crystal warmed.

Kade's voice steadied in the lowline. "Outer ring is closed. Two holes remain. One narrow. One uglier. East is uglier."

"Ugly keeps you standing," Zane said. "We take it."

Mireya's order ran the stone. "Quiet hands. Clean exits. Leave them nothing to count but themselves."

Elia met her gaze. "Then they'll find someone who finally remembers."

CHAPTER 10
HUNTER DRONES

The first death arrived without sirens. It arrived in the hush that follows a held breath.

Sector 3. A fifteen-year-old girl, mid-Harmony Session. The approved lullabies pulsed in the ceiling. Her hum drifted off pattern. Not an anthem. Not even a word. A contour her body remembered. Her mother could not explain where it came from.

They took the girl without notice. No docket. No charge. A door opened, a Band warmed, a face turned patient, the room went quiet. Enforcement wore no insignia. Their machines made no sound. They did not interrogate. They listened—and erased.

News folded itself into a ration manifest, a thin cut that stung only if you pressed the right place. Two hours later: Sector 11. A sanitation foreman paused mid-shift, rubber gloves still slick with cleanser, eyes on a pigeon alighting on a rusted bracket. He said one word to the window. *Freedom.* A drone drifted nearby. The air around him cooled, a pane kissed by winter. He laid down on the tiles as if choosing rest. He did not get up.

By evening, whispers reached a nursery in Sector 8: children telling each other in nap-time voices that a new word lived in their walls. A caregiver pretended not to hear. Her Band warmed. She changed the subject with a smile that showed too many teeth.

None of it entered the Broadcast. The Broadcast declared calm seas, hydration compliance, gratitude for safety so soft people forgot the invoice.

Beneath Sector 19, the report hit Mireya's table hard enough to jolt a tin cup. "Hunter Drones," she said. Her voice stayed low; the room tightened anyway.

The photo was a blur stolen from a satellite latch: dark bodies that suggested wings without granting them, all sensor and intent. Zane folded his arms. "I thought those were a myth."

"Not anymore." Mireya dragged a quick schematic into the grime on the tabletop: sensor ring, acoustic spine, micro-actuators that let the chassis hang motionless in air, a thought about to speak. "AI-piloted. Target-specific. They don't collect, they respond."

Elia's throat knew the information before her mouth formed it. Old certification modules unwound inside her. "Autonomous."

Mireya's mouth thinned. "Memory-sensitive. They track deviation—intonation, emotional lift, the speech your body makes before your tongue does." She touched the drawn sensor. "Hum wrong, speak wrong, feel wrong—tagged."

"And then?" Zane asked, not for knowledge, for witness.

"They shut you off," Mireya said, eyes steady.

The message moved faster than anyone expected. A whisper became a ripple, then a network ache that jumped channels: education templates, dream-therapy overlays, transit ambience, the white noise under cafeteria clatter. Elia's code behaved as designed. It threaded and nested and learned. People started to ask out loud. The Union cut meditation cycles shorter, doubled recalibration hours, swapped vocabulary lists for terms with less air in them. Not enough. The drones filled the gap between doctrine and panic.

In the alcove, Elia tried to slow her head by staring at a child's drawing pinned to a crate wall: a girl next to a tree, sun off-center, letters in oversized wanting strokes—My name is Amara. I love the outside. A confession smuggled over a border. Names had become contraband. So had trees, if your body loved them wrong.

Zane entered without his usual soft step. He wasn't smoothing edges today. "Cell in Sector 6. Three dead. One taken."

She did not ask why. "Because of the message."

He hesitated, a breath that held an argument. "They were listening to the tape. Someone reported."

Guilt turned her stomach by the stem. "This is my fault."

"No," he said, without mercy. "This is their design. You're disrupting it."

She dreamed in wings that night, except there were none. Machines hung in the smooth white the Union preferred, a sky without distance. They did not buzz. They listened. Her mother's voice threaded through the dream the way water finds the low seam.

They aren't afraid of you, Elia. They fear what wakes when you remember.

She woke to a siren that did not belong to the station. It belonged to the grid above. The Harmony cadence tore for a breath long enough to make fillings sing, then knitted. She ran for command. Zane bent over gutted consoles. Mireya had a thumb on the lowline as if the station's pulse sat under her skin.

"Talk to me," Elia said.

"The system's counterpunching," Zane answered. "Black-code tracer on our lattice."

Mireya did not look up. "They have us."

No boots. No bullhorn. No sweet assurances about temporary procedures to ensure public safety. The air changed pressure—the sensation before thunder. Every hair on Elia's arms lifted. Zane's eyes rose from the screen. "Inbound."

"How close?" Mireya asked.

"Four clicks. Low altitude. Tight patterns. Nonhuman control."

"Hunter Drones," Elia said. No one answered because the room had already believed.

The station moved without losing shape. Readiness looked like this after years under siege—habits that had become philosophy. Echo techs split transmitters, calling serials, pairing runners without making predictable pairs. The Flame keepers lifted the physical archive the way you lift both a sleeping baby and explosives—tenderness and terror in one posture. Veils stripped the wall maps, flipped them, and the real routes showed angles that made no sense to a model that valued streets over breaths. A man froze at a corridor mouth, hands hovering, eyes wide. Mireya's voice found his collar and dragged. "Move." He obeyed.

Elia ripped the last memory node out of a maintenance loop she had seeded. If a drone scanned it live, the signature would lead straight back and light a heat map across every safehouse on the lattice. Zane slid in at her shoulder with a rifle that had survived six decades of arguments and learned to cooperate.

"Emergency protocol?" he asked.

"Not yet," Mireya said over lowline, iron under control. "Eyes first. I want to see how they hunt."

At 02:42, a scream rose from the northern access. Not theatrical. A clean human cut sized to fit the exact pain a mouth can measure when reality arrives. Silence. Then a small click. Not mechanical. Internal. The sound of a choice removed.

Zane flipped a feed to a pinhole camera hidden in an inspection light. The image stuttered, cleared. One drone hovered at chest height. Sleek, dark, a refusal to grant a face. The forward plate held a single red ember that pulsed, a fingertip finding a pulse. It did not sweep. It listened.

"Why isn't it moving?" Mireya asked.

"It's measuring fear," Elia said, and heard her voice as a distant girl's.

Zane's head turned a degree. "How do you know?"

"Because that's how you engineer surrender." She hated that her mind still held the blueprints.

The drone surged without warning. Air jumped. The feed dropped to black.

"Evac only," Mireya said, voice gone to wire. "No engagements. If you see one, you run."

The room split along rehearsed fault lines. Veils funneled families into sound-proofed shafts lined with jammers and wool blankets stapled to concrete to fracture sound the way trees fracture wind. Elia should have gone with them.

Zane closed a hand on her forearm. "Not you. With me."

"Where?"

"To finish what you started."

They dropped through a maintenance grate no one would reasonably suspect. Zane had rebuilt the ladder from conduit and an old bed frame. It sang under their boots. Lights above browned and flared—grid load rolling over pain points. Zane's tone stayed steady, the way you speak to someone bleeding without telling them the color. "They're scanning heat. One chance."

The tunnel widened into a relay cavity, a shrine to the possibility of electricity. No Grid tether. No Harmony. No telemetry. A satellite dish shivered ivy from its ribs. Rusted panels waited for touch.

"This still works?" Elia asked.

"I don't think," Zane said, throwing four switches his hands remembered. "I know."

She loaded the fragment she had held back, a key under a brick she knew was hollow. Not a mask. Not a pulse under calm. A voice.

They rewrote your story. They renamed your hope. But I am still here. And so are you. Say it. Say it again. REMEMBER AMERICA.

The relay blinked. The dish remembered turning. The console printed two words without triumph: *Message sent.*

A hum rose in the shaft behind them. It found the back of Elia's teeth. She met Zane's gaze. He did not say run. They were already running.

Boots hammered tile. Walls picked up proximity scans and answered in a soft pulsing red that washed their hands and pulled out their veins as maps. The drone didn't chase on a line. It cut diagonals, closing exits, folding the path toward a cul-de-sac that smelled of old metal and stale water.

"It wants a surrender pocket," Zane said. "Containment field. Your body will do the rest."

"Then we don't give it one." She heard the stubbornness and recognized it—hers, and older than the wipe.

They ducked under a fallen arch. Stone dragged Elia's shoulder, heat, then steadiness. Behind them, the relay climbed a ladder of frequencies—city sats that corrected weather and mood, neighborhood intercoms, public kiosks that printed doctrine, therapy loops, meditation hums, the toneless comfort that fills the seconds when a culture forbids solitude. The words weren't code now. They were said.

They rewrote your story. They renamed your hope. But I am still here. And so are you. Say it. Say it again. REMEMBER AMERICA.

The drone rounded the turn behind them in a motion that told the corridor distance had lied. Too fast. Too near. Zane shoved Elia forward—calculation, not panic. Enough force to move her, not enough to sprawl her. "Go."

"I'm not leaving you." She didn't have to say it. Her body had already refused.

The wall to their right cracked inward. Concrete powdered the air. White-gray blind. The drone slid through the storm, red sensor pinning Elia to tile without touch. A rising chirp traced her frame the way a monk traces air. Heat climbed her spine. Her jaw clenched. Breath learned the mathematics of small.

The old speaker above the relay woke. Not the console. A unit from a time when voices were allowed to guide.

They'll come for the voices first. When they do—don't go quiet. Scream louder. Until your voice becomes someone else's memory.

The drone hesitated. Not long. Long enough. A hiccup in the sensor rhythm as authority channels contradicted kill parameters. The error made space. Zane entered it. He drove a spike charge into the drone's core, thumbed the trigger, and turned his face. Light tore the air. Sound shredded the ear from the inside. The drone folded, limbs tucking, shell collapsing. It struck tile and twitched, red jittering, then died. Smoke wrote small black cursive on stone.

Zane coughed, blood in his grin. "Not bad for a myth." He slumped beside her, hand on ribs, breath even by training and not by fortune.

Elia checked the shape of herself. Everything hurt, nothing failed. "You?"

"Still here." He pushed once against the wall and rose, the motion revealing the cost.

They did not embrace. They moved. The relay pulsed again—a heartbeat in metal.

The words went everywhere. Kitchens where mothers poured nutrient broth into cups that once belonged to grandmothers whose names had never been entered.

Classrooms where children practiced temperate smiles. Factories where hands repeated motions precise enough to be measured into obedience. Quiet apartments where citizens lay in beds designed to cradle correct thoughts. Voices began to answer.

Remember America, a girl told her mirror and did not know she had spoken.

Remember America, a bus driver breathed under the Broadcast's hum and the doors sighed open as if the words bore mass.

Remember America, an old man said to a photograph the grid had blurred again and again until only shape remained, and the shape still meant a face.

In the Civic Core, a technician sat rigid while four indicators flared in a pattern no module had trained him to recognize. His hand rose for a supervisor, then fell when the panel printed *CALM.*

In a Sector 12 stairwell, a boy stopped with a foot on the landing. A nameless pressure pressed through his ribs, requesting entry.

In Sector 8's nursery, a caregiver changed keys mid-hum and did not notice.

Under Sector 19, Mireya stood very still, then crossed the room in three sure steps, issuing orders that sounded more like names for winds than commands. "Echo team, split the drop. Decoy bright. Master in shadow. Joren, runners to Blue. Vault custody: master east intact. Chain holds."

"Custody line holds," an Echo tech repeated, chalk scraping a board no camera saw. "Master east. Decoys north, south."

Kade's voice cut through on lowline from the outer arcs, calm with edges. "Perimeter flares. Pattern drift in the scan band. They're adapting. Change angles every corridor. No repeats."

"Copy," Mireya said. "No habits. We are chaos."

Elia and Zane reentered the main run at a jog that did not announce panic and did not pretend ease. The station's motion reknit around them. Echo techs were already slicing the full broadcast into fragments with bureaucratic names—maintenance advisories, filter updates, counsel empathy checks—and scheduling them to masquerade as inevitable. Veils counted wrists that no longer wore Bands and counted anyway. Joren tried to shape a question about his parents; Mireya answered with a look that meant run now, hope later.

The lowline stitched the map with updates: "Four up." "Nine down." "Outer Belt silent." "Core jittering."

Zane brushed Elia's shoulder—one beat, current through a wire. "Nothing we do matters if we don't get out."

She nodded. Survival was the only permission to keep choosing.

They hit the last junction before the living space and heard it. Not a chant. A seam in silence thinning, the sound a throat makes when it has decided to stop hiding. From far above, faint as a dream you almost hold, a voice spoke and another answered. The answer did not belong to the Union.

Remember America.

Remember America.

Remember America.

Not unity. Not noise. The exact size of a human throat choosing function over safety. Not a chant. A ripple. Not rebellion. Resurrection.

The ripple sprinted. Too fast to track, too wide to constrain. The Broadcast stumbled once, then stood. The cadence returned, thinner. Afraid.

Mireya walked into the corridor with a strip of paper creased into her palm. She set it on the table. Her face gave nothing to the room.

Six words, printed on the Union's emergency override channel:

THE UNION HAS DECLARED WAR ON MEMORY.

Zane exhaled, rough. "So it starts."

Elia pressed her palm to her mother's journal through her jacket. The echo of the last voice rang in her ear bones. She understood, for the first time, the word war without metaphor.

The comms cracked with a merciless voice that had replaced truth with control for so long the substitution sounded normal.

By order of the Harmony Authority, memory is treason.

Red bled through the lights. Doors slammed. Somewhere above, Hunter Drones screamed awake.

Zane's eyes found Elia's. The past she could not name moved in them—left side, three-count, find me even if they change our names—and her own body flashed an answer. A hall under a different city. A hand at her elbow. The same pattern of shield and shove. Her pulse found the old rhythm without consent.

"This is it," he said.

The station erupted. Not panic. Purpose.

◄◄ ► ❚❚ ■ ►►

They did not have the luxury of fresh plans. Only the discipline to keep moving through the ones written into their bones.

Kade fed updated weights from the perimeter, voice a metronome. "Model tilt to audio stress. New feature set:

pulse-lock on fear cadence. Don't give them breath patterns. Stagger steps. Count in fours, break on five."

"Runners, go," Mireya called. "Pairs, but not the pairs you want. Echo, burn the bright decoy and make it embarrassing. Veils, split half with Flame, half with children. If a door argues, apologize later."

Elia and Zane cut through Valve Row. The air held metal and old wet. The test-tone dish Kade had left earlier sang a faint mismatched chord, confusing the model's ear. Zane moved with brutal economy—no elegant arcs, only angles that gave cameras nothing to love. He kept his body on Elia's left without checking. She recognized the geometry before she could think. Her body answered with memory.

Left side. Three-count. Find me even if they rename us.

They reached a mesh curtain. Coins on wire chimed under Zane's knuckles, a dull note that meant clear. He pulled her into a run under the pipes. "Stud to stud," he said. She matched him. Her breath stayed inside her ribs where fear could not find it.

"Dead bulb ahead," he said. "Read quick."

They tucked into the one-meter bite. The bulb glowed without speaking to any network. Zane cupped her hands with his, steadying them around the strip she had pulled from the red spine. The gesture lasted one breath. It said more than a paragraph.

He unfolded the paper.

To speak, use memory's bones.

Three drawn taps. Arrow to left margin.

Her eyebrow twitched where a thumb had pressed once. Tap. Tap. Tap. The world doubled for a beat. Not déjà vu. A seam rubbing raw where two lives tried to line.

Footsteps brushed stone two corridors over. Soft. Measured. The sound an AI makes when it borrows human rhythm. Zane refolded the strip and placed it in her palm. "Keep it on you."

Joren slid into view, breath held to stay quiet. "Vault custody confirms," he whispered. "Master east intact. Decoys set. North runner through. South runner late."

"Go meet him," Mireya's voice ordered through lowline. "Nobody dies guarding paper."

A hum passed across the ceiling—a scan sweeping for a fear pulse. Elia counted on fours and broke on five. The hum slid past, hungry for steadier music.

They moved. The model adapted. It cut off routes a human would choose. It sniffed for fresh habit. Zane changed angle at every turn. Kade's voice kept time. "No repeats. Count on prime numbers. Make it ugly."

The station became an instrument. People struck the right wrong notes. The model missed by inches, learned, corrected, missed again. The air felt charged, a storm deciding which house to spare.

They reached the junction that led to the old wash station, the place you pass to reach the archive door. Elia felt the pull to turn and check on the books. Zane must have felt it in her shoulder. His hand tightened pressure that said not yet.

A shadow moved across the cross-corridor. Not a person. The intelligence in the motion boxed corners and then emptied them. Zane cursed under his breath. "Back." They slid into an alcove no wider than a sigh. The drone drifted past. The red pulse on its forward plate flared and dimmed, listening for human music. It stilled. Not hunting a body. Hunting the memory inside it.

Elia's breath wanted to match Zane's. He broke his pattern by one beat. Her lungs followed. The sensor did not wake.

For three breaths they did not exist. The drone moved on, unbothered by the physics of weight.

Zane tipped his chin. "Go."

They slid to the opposite wall and crossed the mouth of the corridor at a diagonal that gave the camera geometry nothing to file. The door to the archive sat three pillars down. Mireya stood there, shoulders square, eyes level. Behind her, Flame lifted boxes with the care of surgeons who know the patient will wake if their hands falter.

Mireya did not waste a word. "We hold long enough to empty this room, or we never forgive ourselves." Her palm brushed Elia's sleeve, the smallest permission. "Take what you can carry that will matter to someone who hasn't met us."

Elia took the first thing that met her hand without preciousness. A thin book of songs repaired with kitchen thread. A name in block letters on the inside corner, the child's hand that had written it now at least a decade older. She tucked it into her jacket. Zane slid a book into his pack without looking at the title. The motion wore tenderness the way a tool wears polish—work and time, not softness.

Kade's voice spiked on lowline. "Core outriders at the east vents. Model updated. It learned our test tone. It wants cadence. Give it silence. Then give it noise."

Mireya's jaw set. "Time."

Flame passed the last crate through the seam. Veils sealed the panel without a squeal. The archive vanished back into stone.

"Go," Mireya said. "Every second after this one cost double."

They scattered down three different throats. Zane kept Elia on his left. The corridor narrowed. A vent exhaled heat and oil. The drone sound came again, the glass-song that finds teeth. Zane stopped so fast Elia almost ran into him.

He put a hand out without looking, found her sternum, steadied. The gesture should have been nothing. It burned.

A memory broke surface—Zane's hand in the same place, another city, other walls, the same three-count through her ribs before a sprint. She had no picture. Only the certainty of a shape she had occupied before. Her mouth filled with the metallic taste of someone else's name for her own life and then cleared. The drone drifted past, hunting a different fear.

They moved. The station thinned to only the words that mattered. Clear. Close. Wait. Now. Left. Up. Hold. Go.

At the outer throat, the world opened to stale night, ducts huffing, a sky the color of milk burned. Voices brushed the edges of air—far off, strangers repeating a phrase as if testing a stair tread for strength. *Remember America.* The sound did not gather. It multiplied.

They ran the last stretch bent low under a line of pipes that sweated condensation into a tin pan that had been placed there before either of them had arrived in this life. Zane checked the corner with a mirror, the size of a card. Clear.

Joren appeared from the stairwell, cheeks hollowed, eyes blown wide and somehow steady. "South runner through," he said. "He dropped the decoy on purpose. Let it get caught. Smiled at the camera."

Zane's mouth set. "Names later."

"Names later," Joren echoed, and peeled off to the left with a pouch of transmitters against his chest.

They reached the final access and stopped. The corridor ahead was empty. Too empty. The air held the attention of a predator that knows you know it is there.

Zane leaned to Elia's ear. "On my call—no heroics."

"When have I—"

He cut her off with one word. "Please."

He threw a bolt at the far wall. The drone revealed itself—not by sound, by negation. Space became intention. Red flared. The machine drifted from a pocket of air you would not have noticed until it decided to become real.

Elia's body started to sprint. Zane's hand checked her chest again, then lifted, open palm to her heart, a beat in time with the three drawn taps on the paper in her pocket. Tap. Tap. Tap. The signal they had buried in each other long before memory loss.

"Now," he said.

They went. The drone sliced the corner late by breath, recalculating in a math that had never needed to solve for two humans moving on a rhythm older than the algorithm. They reached the next seam and slid through. Zane wedged the panel without squeal. The red pulse washed over stone on the other side, hunting a breath that had already moved.

Down the ladder. Across a sump. Up another rung where the welds showed three hands' worth of different skill. The station's hum fell behind them.

The city above vibrated at a new pitch. Windows glowed without warmth. The Broadcast sounded normal, which made the fear worse. Elia and Zane ran the shadowed strip between two dead buildings and dropped into an intake that had not been mapped since maps had stopped admitting cities were built by people.

They stopped only when Mireya's voice in their ears said one word. "Hold."

They held. Not from exhaustion. From instruction.

The comms boomed, a voice that had replaced language with control for years and trained throats to accept it.

By order of the Harmony Authority, memory is treason.

The night answered. A thousand throats in a hundred rooms said a single sentence that did not ask permission.

"Remember America."

No siren followed. Only the new pitch of fear from the machines that had believed themselves the only singers in this city.

Zane's hand found Elia's again for one beat, then withdrew. He did not look at her. He did not need to. The pattern between them burned with certainty.

"This is it," he said.

CHAPTER 11
THE BROADCAST VIRUS

They hit the hub still tasting stone.

Dust sheeted off their jackets when they shouldered through the curtain. The world in here kept moving because stopping was something the Union could measure toggles clicked, fans sawed air, the relay stack breathed its soft animal heat. Zane scanned the corners without thinking—doors, vents, wrists, eyes—and only then looked at Elia. "You good?"

"Good enough." The answer was steady. The skin along her cheek sang from a near kiss with hot metal. Her hands remembered the slit under her palms. Her mouth remembered a voice that had used her name as if it owned it.

Mireya didn't turn all the way toward them. She lifted a hand and Kade swept a no-light sweep: headlamps dead, optics taped, jammers thinned to a rustle. "Cold," Kade said after a beat. "No live pings tailing."

Elia rolled her shoulder once, dropped to a console, and laid her fingers on the casing to feel it hum. The room's heat came up through the metal into her skin like a held note. She could hear the echo of what they'd sent still ricocheting in the lattice; not code, not command—memory where it wasn't supposed to live.

"Report," Mireya said.

Joren—hair matted, chest working too fast—rattled it off. "Sector 4's repeating. Sector 8's splintering—kids whispering at nap, caregivers pretending not to hear. Sector 2 went stiff when the phrase hit a kitchen radio. Three drones over District 2 at roofline; low enough to feel."

"Too obvious," Zane said. "They want to be seen."

"For once," Mireya answered. Not approval.

A runner at the door breathed permission only when she pointed. "Station C says the cache is lagging. They need a manual reset."

Elia felt the hub's hum hitch in her bones. Lag meant the seed could dull. Lag meant the lattice started smoothing, the way water smooths a stone you meant to keep sharp.

"Send Calia," Zane said.

"Calia's on the upper vent. We can't pull her." Mireya's gaze landed and stayed. "Elia."

"I'll go."

Zane's mouth shaped a protest that didn't get air.

"Take him," Mireya added, meaning Zane. "You'll need someone to fit the hinge."

They were already moving when the hub screens hiccupped and flushed pale. A voice slid into the room like a practiced hand into a glove.

Good afternoon, citizens.

They stopped. The air thinned.

The face on the screen was no face at all, just a slate-blue seal that meant Authority and the square, forgiving serif of the Harmony Authority. The voice was low, clinical, constructed like a cradle.

In periods of heightened recollection, the nervous system may experience semantic noise. The Authority has opened Memory Clinics in each sector to help you rest your minds. Harmony begins when memory rests. Stray recollection is noise. To be well is to release.

No insignia. No threat words. The phrasing moved like water and wore the cadence of care.

Mireya's face went still in the way that meant fury.

The seal cut to a room: light that looked like mercy, a chair that looked like apology, a clinician with eyes the color of steel thinking about rain. The clinician folded her hands, palms visible, as if to show the city she wasn't holding a weapon.

If you have recently experienced unhelpful remembrance, come in. We will ease it.

The voice shifted. Not enough for anyone else to hear. Enough for Elia to feel like a thread being tugged inside her chest. A single, sweetened cadence—half a syllable— slipped the way her mother had slipped the word remember when she wanted it to travel.

Elia swallowed. Zane's head turned a fraction, clocking the micro-flinch he wasn't supposed to see. He said nothing. He moved closer by a degree that read as nothing to a camera and as a shelter to a person.

Mireya cut the feed with a knife of a finger. "He's in the room," she said to no screen. "He just isn't using the door."

Zane exhaled through his teeth. "Carrow."

No one said yes. No one had to.

"Move," Mireya told them. "Reset C. Then we decide if we burn or build."

They took the tunnel at a run. The station breathed damp and iron. Pipes shouldered the ceiling. Light pooled dirty yellow, which was good—yellow didn't carry far when you didn't want to be found. Zane slipped into his half step ahead, then checked it, letting her pass the pinch first, a habit he would call tactics in daylight and a kind of love in the dark. She slid into his blind side without thinking, and he noticed that too, the way his gaze clicked, then eased.

"You okay?" he asked when the floor sloped and the air got thinner, then thick, as if the station had decided breathing was a job it might not want to do.

"Phase Black doesn't have okay." It came out dry. He huffed a laugh that didn't find humor.

They reached the grate. Zane knelt and set the hook into the bad weld like he'd been the one to lay it; he probably had. "Hold," he said. "It will want to drop when the catch goes."

She took the weight and felt the teeth of the steel carve a tread into her skin. He worked the lip, breath quiet at her shoulder, the clean wrongness of Union cleanser on his jacket ghosting under leather and heat.

The catch let go. They set the grate down on a breath, no bang, just metal thinking about sound and deciding against it. The crawlspace beyond yawned black. Cables hung like tendon. Cold rolled out. Elia went in first because that was the order of the world and because the only way to quiet the static under her skin was to use her body.

The duct narrowed until ribs counted the inches for them. Their breaths became a call and answer they hadn't agreed to and couldn't help. At the junction box she found the latch with fingers smaller than his. Dust coughed into her face and his hand found the small of her back once, just once, not claiming, only anchoring.

She reset the relay. Dead-red blinked to truer green, one by one like streetlamps down an empty road. The lattice hiccupped in her ear—then cleared.

"C back up," she whispered.

"Clean," Joren breathed in her bead. "Clean. Okay."

They stayed a beat longer than necessary, not because the work needed it, because they did. The duct smelled faintly of old rain, as if it remembered something it was no longer allowed to be near. Elia shifted and felt Zane's arm along hers. If she turned her head, her mouth would find his jaw. She didn't. They moved. The station kept them like valuables in its pockets and carried them back to the heat.

◄◄ ► ❚❚ ■ ►►

"Rotate the uplink fifteen degrees every eight minutes," Mireya said when they slid back into the hub, not looking up from a schematic that had stopped being theoretical and started being a map of the next hour of their lives. "Stagger with dead-pulse. Make it look like sewage vent interference."

Kade's fingers walked. Joren's foot tapped in a pattern that meant I'm listening faster than you can speak. Elia rethreaded the line and felt for the dip where the counter-phrase had been stitched into the city's daily breath. She didn't name it herself yet. She felt it in her teeth.

The hub throbbed like a buried heart. Not loud— shallow, relentless. Elia pared the noise of it down to three truths she could hold. The fan on rack two stuttered on every third spin. The lowline cracked at the consonants when someone breathed too close to the mouthpiece. The uplink's light changed color if you looked at it with your head tilted—blue from one angle, violet from another—as if reminding you that nothing was only what it said.

"Clinic vans are rolling," Joren reported, voice tightening. "No sirens. They're pinging bands for wellness checks. Pull-in times under eight minutes."

Elia's mouth went dry. She had stood in those vans once; a life they had trained out of her. She remembered the smell: citrus and sugar and something that made the back of the throat numb. She had called it compliance then and got a commendation. Now the word turned to iron on her tongue.

"They won't use force," Mireya said, eyes on the board. "They'll use relief."

Zane's fists opened and closed. "Our people have learned to be grateful for the absence of pain." He glanced at Elia; the line he didn't say hung between them—people before tapes—and then he said it out loud, not to her, to the room. "We save people before tapes."

The argument that had been waiting in the lungs of the hub came out in a controlled exhale.

"Full drop now," someone said—Echo tech, scarred knuckles, the kind of man who had survived by being louder than machines. "They're saying it out loud, Zane. Finish it."

Another voice: "Long game. They'll snuff a blaze. We keep them finding ash."

No shouting. Mireya didn't allow shouting. Clarity only.

Elia didn't speak. In her head a pair of lines braided: *They will call you dangerous before they call you true.*

Vault, then custody.

"How long until the counter-phrase smooths our baseline?" Kade asked, not looking at anyone, eyes on the trace.

"It's already smoothing," Elia said. She didn't have to open the code to know. She could hear it in the way the city breathed. "They're training a counter-baseline."

"Then we need the weights," Zane said. "And their inoculation profile."

"HighHub," Mireya said. The word made everyone in the room smaller, not because the room got bigger, because the HighHub sat above them like a thought you didn't want to finish.

"Maintenance tier," Kade added. "Mirror node. We don't have to touch core. In and out with the strain. I can ride you a pattern."

Mireya drew the decision in a single line across the air. "Elia. Zane. Joren. Kade on ops. Joren runs. Kade sings. I hold. No-light sweep out and in. If you have to choose between perfect data and an open evac corridor—"

"People," Zane said. He didn't look at Elia. He didn't have to. The glance was already there. They moved.

◄◄ ► ❚❚ ■ ►►

Night pulled the streets thin, and the city hummed in a key it used when it wanted to forgive itself. They kept to the throat between buildings where heat pooled and bands before they'd been ripped off used to stutter. Above them, windows glowed the color of blank paper. A tram whispered past without passengers. In a barber shop, a chair stood turned just so, as if a man had been called mid-cut and told a better story had arrived elsewhere. In a dialysis ward, machines blinked their metronomes around an old woman's body, and she whispered the word remember to the ceiling and the ceiling didn't answer but the skin along her arms found itself.

Joren took point, shoulders set like a door. Kade's voice lived in Elia's ear—numbers without panic. "Two nodes chatting at G-15. Clinic van at West Loop. They're overfitting to HRV, expecting fear. Give them boredom."

"Shame we didn't pack a sermon," Zane murmured.

The HighHub rose like a cured bone. The maintenance tier breathed coolant and old rain. They slipped along a gantry that trembled under their feet as if remembering different hands. A drone drifted across from the far side, lens tasting the air. Not a sweep. A pause. Listening.

Zane's palm opened, three fingers ready to count. Elia moved on the third before he said the three. He blinked, the smallest intake of breath. His mouth didn't smile. Something else did. Recognition widened by a degree and then trimmed itself smaller for safety.

They pressed flat behind a dead bulb. No talk. The drone hung. It adjusted not to sight, to micro-tremor, the flutter of skin you can't discipline when a memory walks up to your ribs and knocks. Elia breathed the way she had trained herself in the duct—down and wide, flattening the wave until her body signed normal to a machine that didn't deserve that trust. Beside her, Zane counted along her breath without asking for it; he'd tuned to her pace without knowing when.

The drone drifted on. Its path wasn't random. Kade's whisper confirmed it: "They're herding. Adapting in real time. We're not prey; we're models."

"Good," Zane said. "Models have parameters."

The service door gave to a shape of pressure Zane had taught his hands years ago. Inside, the maintenance mirror wore a borrowed face: an old pediatric rack shell, a hairstreak of peeling sticker along the edge. Elia's fingers slid over the panel and found the seam nobody believed in unless they had seen a seam open once and realized the world kept secrets you couldn't smell.

She plugged in. The code rose like a flock and banked.

Not a lot of words, Elia told herself. Show, then name it once.

She didn't scroll. She listened. The inoculation grammar moved like a balm across a burn—measured, pseudo-kind.

Harmony begins when memory rests. Stray recollection is noise. To be well is to release.

It threaded itself through mediation loops, nutrition pop-ups, transit chimes, clinic wait-music. Not loud. Everywhere.

And beneath it the weights: matrices assigning risk to pairs, triples, syllables arranged like beads on a string, safe unless you knew how to cut the right place and let the beads fall into a new shape. The counter-baseline had been trained off their first wave. She had expected it to be cold. It wasn't. It was careful. That made it worse.

Her hands remembered a workbench that had never belonged to the Union and a man's shoulder that had crowded hers on purpose so she knew he trusted her to bump back. She had brought this into the world and the Union had stolen the syntax and renamed it medicine. Rage ran electric up her arms and cooled when it hit her fingers; heat didn't fix things. She did.

"Vault the weights," she said, voice calm in her own ears. "Vault, then custody. Two copies only. No mirrors in hub memory. Runners move in pairs."

"Copy," Zane said, hand already at the pocket seam where his jacket hid a sleeve that had saved three lives this month by being easy to miss.

Joren held the pouch like eggs and slid the first shard into the felt, the second into its twin. "Custody one," he said, touching the pouch with two fingers. He passed the twin to Zane. "Custody two."

Kade's whisper sharpened. "Hold. Anomaly."

Elia froze without stopping her hands. "Where?"

"HighHub node C-Delta shows a null. Not down. Empty."

"A blind," Zane said.

"For us," Kade said. "Or for anyone who steps where we just stepped."

Elia rewrote their handshake to look like wear in a cable that had been used to carry maintenance traffic in the old city when people still believed pipes could be honest. The mirror accepted it like a sigh.

"We've got it," Zane said. "Out."

They moved, the path back making more noise in their heads than their feet ever would. On the gantry, a Clinic van drifted into view through the lattice of pipes outside the skin of the building. Inside the van, citizens sat with their hands folded for absence of guilt; a clinician smiled with professional mercy and said, *release,* and the Band on a man's wrist pulsed relief like a drug.

Two vignettes only, Elia told herself, because her mind wanted to gather the entire city and wrap it in a sentence it would believe. A bus door huffed open, and the driver stared into the dark as if the dark had changed its mind about being empty. A daycare radio hummed a tune one half-step off and a child's nap breath matched it, then refused to.

They hit the stairs. Kade's voice came thin and hard as wire. "Stop. Quarantine your copy. The mirror has a—hell—double backtrace."

"What did it tag?" Zane asked, body already between Elia and the stairwell mouth, not gallant, tactical.

"Not you." Kade's breath hitched. "The second the weights touched our lattice, the backtrace opened a maintenance ticket in a public health submesh and the submesh queued a wellness review. It fired not here—home grid. Joren—"

Joren's face drained to chalk. "Sector 3," he said, voice small in a body full of speed. "My parents."

Elia felt the decision drop into the room with the weight of an anvil. People or tapes. It wasn't theoretical if it had names.

"Quarantine holds," Kade said fast, guilt quick as lightning behind the words even if it wasn't his to carry. "We sealed it after the first ping. But the first was enough. The Clinic is en route. No siren."

Zane didn't waste air on blame. He cut the space into parts. "Mireya—"

"Get out," Mireya said in their ears, voice as flat as a blade laid on a table. "Bring me the weights and the profile. We'll decide the rest when I see your faces."

They ran. The city changed as they moved, or maybe they were only looking differently, the way you see color once someone tells you it has a name. Drones didn't hunt streets. They hunted responses. The counter-phrase ate the edges off fear; the Clinics took what remained, softening it into something you could call consent in a report.

At the mouth of an alley, a drone hung at chest height and didn't move. It listened. Zane's fingers lifted to count. Elia moved on his rhythm like a body that had done this before with this man, and it shook him for half a second the way a door shakes if you pull it the wrong way and it still opens.

The hub reeked like hot copper and lentils. Mireya stood with her hands on the table as if touch might hold the board in place. Zane laid the shard in her palm. Joren set the pouch beside it like an offering. His mouth was a straight line he'd cut there himself.

"Vault," Mireya said. The sparrow-throated tech ghosted in to take the shards. "Custody two stays with me until we split. We mirror nowhere."

"Counter-phrase?" Kade asked.

Elia pushed the clinic profile and weights onto the local and kept her own copy off the lattice. "They're training off our first wave. They're teaching the city to call recollection fatigue and fatigue medicine."

"Can you tune us around it?"

"Yes. But we lose surface if I make it safe." She met Zane's eyes. "People, not perfection."

He held her gaze and nodded, small. The glance you wrote into the plan—people over tapes—landed without fanfare. They were already living it.

The screens stuttered. The seal returned. Not the clinician this time. The voice that had opened the city in two and asked it to call the wound wellness.

Citizens. We hear your fatigue. We see your strain. We will help you release the extra weight of memory.

Carrow stepped into frame with no name under his. He didn't need one. He wore the kind of face that had practiced looking like a mirror until other people saw themselves and forgot to ask who was holding the glass.

"The Harmony Authority exists to make sure you do not carry more than is useful. Your well-being is our mission. There is no punishment here. Only care."

He smiled. It didn't touch the eyes. Then he made the mistake. It was nothing, and it was everything. He quoted an old civic motto—"We remember the best of us"—and the *we* hit the air with the half-note curl Elia's mother had used when she wanted a word to reach the bones of a child across a room full of noise.

Elia's stomach went cold. Zane felt the flinch in the air if not on her skin and stepped half a step closer, politically, tactically, personally. Carrow continued with care that looked like kindness.

"If someone you love is struggling with unhelpful remembrance, bring them to a Clinic. Or call. We will come. This is not an arrest. This is relief."

The feed cut.

"No sirens," Mireya said softly. "No chains. They'll make people thank them."

Joren stood very straight, as if posture could hold his family up across districts. "Sector 3," he said. He didn't say Mom. He didn't say Dad. The words would make it harder for the room to choose.

Elia laid both palms on the casing and listened to the system breathe through them. The counter-baseline moved like hands smoothing a blanket over a face. She set stones into the river of it and bent the current. Small stones. Enough. She taught a counseling script how to carry the word under a different cadence, a transit chime how to miss a pitch just enough to itch the ear, a nutrition prompt how to put remember two syllables lower so it would wake in sleep.

"Send the first retune," Mireya said.

They sent it. The hub's pitch changed by the thickness of a hair. Kade's face went slack with the kind of relief that only ever lasts two breaths.

The lowline clicked. Not their click. A public channel bled through before Kade snuffed it: "Sector 3 Wellness Unit en route. Subject family name: — " The label blurred on purpose. The grid had decided to be kind.

Joren made no sound. Silence climbed his body like water.

"Go," Zane said, not to Joren, to Mireya. "We can get them."

Mireya's mouth didn't move and still said no. "We hold the lattice. We send them a path to refuse care and not be noticed. We are not a rescue unit. We are not enough guns to win daylight."

"People," Zane said again, raw.

"People," Mireya agreed. "Which is why you hold this and make sure twenty families breathe tomorrow instead of one."

The last word hung between the three of them like a dropped wire.

Elia didn't look at Zane. She looked at Joren. "Tell me their route," she said. "Which Clinic. Which cross. Which elevator. I'll sew noise into it. I will make the band read sleep if they keep very still."

Joren blinked once, twice, as if deciding not to break were a skill you had to warm up. "Corner of Fifth and Low. They always use the Lower East intake. Mom won't argue. Dad will try to be polite."

"Good," Elia said. "Polite reads lower HRV. Polite buys us seconds."

Kade's hands moved. "I can fake a sewer hiccup at the Four/Low transformer. Vents cough. Clinic van shaves time to avoid smell. They reroute. We get a window at the long light."

Mireya tipped her chin. "Do it."

Zane turned his face so only the table saw the shape of his mouth. He was a better man than the city deserved because he said nothing about the math of one family against a map of districts and still found a way to keep standing.

They pushed the second retune. The lattice took it grudgingly then greedy, like thirst pretending it wasn't before it drinks. Elia watched the counter-baseline shiver, recalculating itself and stepping into the new shape with the brisk guiltless efficiency of a system that believes in results more than people.

"Clinic van approaching intersection," Kade said. "Cueing sewer. Three—two—vent cough."

In her ear the city cleared its throat. The van hummed forward, adjusting its course around an odor nobody wanted to report. Elia slid a lull under the intake door chime. It landed exactly where she'd aimed—in the part of the brain that keeps a person from starting a fight in a waiting room. She hated herself a little for using it. She used it anyway.

"Window," Kade whispered. "Two minutes fifty."

Elia spoke into the quiet of her bead, not a command, a story. "Mrs. Joren, if anyone asks, you are tired and you want to drink water. Mr. Joren, you are thinking about your father's favorite song but you won't say which, because you don't quite remember. When they say release, you think about lifting a bag from someone's hand. You don't let go of the hand, only the bag."

Joren pressed his fingers so hard into the edge of the table they went pale, then pink.

"Forty seconds," Kade said. "Long light."

Elia lifted her hand from the casing as if her touch had weight and would drag the city off balance if she kept it there. In her head, for no reason her training would accept, an image arrived: her mother's hands tying a knot behind a child's neck so a paper crown would stay through the party and not feel heavy. She put the image down where she kept sharp things so it would cut if she needed it.

"Van cleared the light," Kade breathed. "Split at Low. The Clinic's bored. Bands read calm. We bought time."

Joren let out a sound that wasn't relief and wasn't pain. It was the sound of a boy who had agreed not to break breaking in a way only he could hear.

The board blinked twice. The feed jumped. A maintenance crawler's camera stuttered and gave them an angle nobody had paid for: a school staircase, a mural peeling in curls. A teacher's arm out, the specific geometry of a woman deciding not to move from a threshold where the world splits children from what they don't get to see. A drone slid into frame without sound and without insignia. Elia felt the room lean toward it like bodies learning to fear a shape.

Mireya paused the frame and set it down very gently. "They're doing it in daylight," she said. "In front of children. Our message gave people a question. The Union bought itself permission to answer with demonstration."

"We don't have enough to hit that stair," Zane said. He wasn't arguing with anyone. He was arguing with physics.

"We have enough to keep her from being the only act of courage in the building," Mireya said. "That's what we use enough for."

The lowline snapped again, riding an edge, it hadn't earned. "Transit Vein query: Sector 19. Vantage required." The voice in their ears did not belong to a clinician or a drone. It belonged to someone who had decided to speak in the city's mother tongue.

"Carrow," Zane said.

Mireya didn't say yes. She didn't have to. She looked at Elia. "He's not calling Enforcement. He's calling public health. He will come in as care. He will go out as whatever he came in to find."

Elia's throat felt lined with paper she hadn't meant to swallow. "How close?"

"Three grids," Kade said. "Outer Belt is hot. He's tasting the vein."

Zane stepped in until hub noise fell away by a hair. "We move you south. There's a stuck door in the crawl. Honest door."

"I'm not a package," Elia said. The humor that arrived surprised both of them.

"No," he said. "You're the fuse."

"Wires carry current," she said. "People carry meaning."

His eyes changed focus as if a lens slipped into truer alignment. "Then let's keep you carrying."

"Third retune?" Mireya asked, already knowing.

Elia touched the casing. The city's breath came through it, mixed now with something like a shiver. She bent the counter-baseline to one more degree, enough to keep the Clinics from finding every throat that had learned to say the word out loud in a kitchen. Not perfect. Alive.

"Third wave's clean," Kade said, brittle.

Mireya nodded once, letting herself sit in the chair for the first time since the night went white. "Go," she said. "South crawl. If you hear the drones, do not run. If you hear Carrow, do not speak."

"What if he speaks to me?" Elia asked before she could stop herself.

"Don't give him the courtesy of your voice," Mireya said. "He doesn't deserve it."

They left without touching because touching would spend something they needed later. The corridor narrowed, exhaled cold. The door sulked in its frame, paint lifting in patient curls. Zane set his shoulder gently. The door reconsidered and gave an inch.

They slid into the crawl. Metal bit the air like a bitten tongue. Zane let the latch kiss the frame behind them and the seam glowed a pinpoint red. The dot jittered, fixed, widened.

"Down," Zane hissed, already hauling her sideways when the seam detonated inward with a pop and a slice of white. The drone's acoustic spine screamed; the screws in the junction box shivered; her teeth went thin as glass. Dust went up. Cables snapped.

Elia slid, forearms burning, as the lens searched and found heat. A second pulse branded the floor where her ribs had been. Zane tossed a tool; it pinged off the housing, buying the kind of breath you count in quarter seconds. The shaft kinked left into tighter dark. They took it.

The lattice in her ear flared without permission—public health bandwidth bled through, a voice wearing empathy like a lab coat. "Sector 19—mark the south crawl." Then, astonishingly, intimately: "Elia."

Her name in that mouth shrank the world to one choice. Zane braced under a slit too small for men who wanted to get out fast. "There," he said, ragged. "Up."

She planted, pushed, tore rust, shoved again. Night air knifed in—wet city, old rain.

Behind them the drone forced its shell through the wound and fired. The shock shaved a bolt past her cheek. Heat kissed skin. She flinched to the side and saw the dot slide, picking Zane's spine like a door it had the code for.

She didn't think. She dropped back and dragged his collar hard enough to rip stitches when the pulse ate the space where his lungs had been. The slit screamed metal. Concrete shifted under their knees. The station groaned.

A new voice rode the ruin. Not the clinician. Not Carrow.

If they come for the voices first, don't go silent. Scream louder...

Her mother.

The drone's lens hiccupped. Not long. Long enough for Zane to slam a spike into its core. Light. Sound like foil tearing inside the skull. The drone folded in on itself, legs tucking, dot jittering, then dark.

They didn't celebrate. They breathed. They crawled. They broke into air so cool it felt like theft.

Behind them, the crawl cauterized. Before them, the street didn't know what had just almost happened and still they could feel the city trying to name it—the way a body tries to name pain so it can call the right person.

Their beads cracked with Kade's voice, thin as wire pulled too tight. "Joren—Clinic van stalled by the light at Low. Your dad made a joke about soup. The clinician laughed. They're bored. You have a window. You can get there if—"

Mireya cut in, iron. "No. We hold."

Joren's breath hit the channel and didn't go in all the way.

"We have the weights," Kade said, almost begging the facts to be enough. "We have the profile. We have a tune."

And then the room went quiet not because anyone chose quiet, because the public channel bled again without asking permission. A soft chime. A text like mercy.

Memory Clinic appointment confirmed. Sector 3 Family Unit: Joren.

Elia pressed her palm to the slick steel of a door that had been honest enough to stick and felt the world pick a shape.

Zane turned his head toward her, or maybe toward what they had made in a duct, and didn't touch because they had already used that kind of language today and you don't repeat yourself when everyone is listening.

"What do we do?" Joren asked, naked and not a boy.

Mireya looked at the board that mapped a city she had not promised to save.

"We answer now," she said. "And we pay for it immediately."

The lowline cracked again. Carrow's voice—warm, mechanic of the soul—stepped into the same room as their breath.

"Neighbors of Sector 3—if someone you love is struggling with unhelpful remembrance, open your door. We're here to help."

The lights didn't change color. No siren bit down. Somewhere a bus driver put both hands on a wheel. Somewhere a child hummed the wrong tune and fell silent because a clinician smiled.

Zane looked at Elia. "People," he said. He didn't make it a question.

Elia thought of a kitchen radio older than reason, a daycare nap, a boy holding a note behind a door that smelled like sugar, a mother's voice wired into a hunt. She thought of Joren's father trying to be polite. She thought of a sentence that had already chosen to live without their permission.

"People," she said.

Then everything that could move moved at once.

ERASURE

E lia."
Her mother's voice bled through the Union channel like a fever dream you cannot wake from. The seam in the south crawl glowed to a red pupil, widened, and popped inward. White knifed the dark.

"Run," Zane said. He hauled her sideways.

They tore into weather like a wet knife. Night took them in fast breaths. A ladder. A grate that gave under boot. Air that tasted of old rain and burned plastic. Behind them the crawl screamed. A drone forced its shell through stone. The sound lived inside teeth more than ears.

They burst into an alley washed in emergency light. Above, the Pulse Net hiccupped. Then the city forgot to make noise.

Not the soft hush the Union sells. A raw vacuum. One held breath. Windows kept their own counsel. Rails thinned to a whisper. Panels blinked dumb and dark.

For a heartbeat, it looked like mercy. Every Band lit white.

SIGNAL INTERFERENCE DETECTED
REMAIN CALM
DO NOT QUESTION

The warning burned across glass and skin at once. Elia pictured hands jerking back. Wrists seared under the light. That little flinch when a lie touches bone. Questions spidered through the silence.

"What happened?"

"Why now?"

"What is wrong with the Grid?"

In Sector 4 a drone descended over the Harmony Fountain. It did not dive. It hung, sure of itself, stirring the water into circles that never closed. The red sensor blinked. A small voice near the basin asked, "What is it doing?" The plinth speaker answered in velvet monotone that had never belonged to a human mouth.

ZONE IS COMPROMISED
EMOTIONAL VARIANCE DETECTED
INTITIATING CORRECTION

The pulse lived under hearing and inside bones. Bodies folded in sequence. Knees, then shoulders. Heads bowed as if told to pray.

They ran bent to shadow. They slid along gutters where foam gathered. Zane counted turns. Elia matched him without thinking. Her body kept a count it had not known it knew. Joren ghosted them from the right with a slate hugged to his ribs. They dropped into a service culvert and fell into the Station's throat. The air tightened. Wet copper and hot dust over wire rubbed thin.

Mireya stood at the hub mouth with her hair shoved back by a hand that had not been gentle.

"Pairs only," she said. The calm had an edge that cut if you leaned. "No singles. Rotate routes on my signal. If a path repeats, it is burned."

Joren pressed his palm to the plate. His voice climbed through hacked intercoms and stairwells and shop basements. It ran like clean thread through dirty air.

"This is Joren," he said. No codename. "If you can hear me, breathe with me. Four in. Four out. If your Band burns, cool it with water, do not rip. If you can, write a name. Hide it in your shoe. If you cannot write, say it under your breath. Names hold."

His words moved through kitchens and halls. A hand on a back. Stand.

Screens shivered. The hub's panel spat stolen feeds that would not hold. Elia stood inside the heat of the servers with her palms set on the casing until the pitch settled under her skin. The message she had sown glowed along the lattice like a vein that refused to close. The Union answered with water cannons and something colder.

Mireya marked three streets with the side of a pencil. "Memory Clinics are rolling." The words landed like a door shutting. "Soft detainments. They arrive as home health. They do not record. They change what you can feel."

"Counter-phrase?" Zane asked.

Elia heard it as he did. Under the public scroll, a new line threaded the air. An inoculation.

HARMONY IS HOME
HOME IS QUIET
QUIET IS CARE

It tried to sit where her mother's sentence had lived. It did not fit.

"We ride over it," Elia said. "No debate. Memory shows."

"Two minutes," Mireya said. "Then we move." She did not look at Elia when she added, "Your call."

Mara Vale's face flashed on a feed. Pixel-sick. Brave. Late. "You don't own my mind. You don't own my past. My name is Mara Vale. And I remember." The feed cut to snow. A fan somewhere ticked once and lied about being fine.

"She knew they were coming," Elia said. Her voice stayed level. "She said it anyway."

"You want the full drop," Mireya said.

"Yes," Elia said. "No more polite. Not fragments. The tape. All of it."

"Under fire," Zane said. It sounded like a warning until she saw his eyes. It was a vow.

"Under fire," she said.

Above, the city adjusted its teeth.

A nurse in a velvet-blue jacket held a hand over an old woman's burned Band. "Think of the beach," a wall speaker told her. The words had been routed to soothe the caregiver more than the patient. The nurse's mouth obeyed.

Her eyes did not. They filled and hardened. Under the script she hummed three off-key notes. The old woman shaped a name she had been told to forget. The drone dipped from the ceiling. The nurse stopped humming and smiled the required smile. She walked out and vomited in a sink full of dispensers.

A bus driver in Sector 12 kept both hands on the wheel. His Band flared white. He whispered to glass that had stopped being a window years ago. "Remember America." He flinched as if he had broken something. Nothing did. The bus stopped where it was told. Passengers traded places. No one held another's gaze.

Back in the hub, Mireya slid Elia toward the mic with two fingers. "Are you sure?"

Elia nodded. Choice mattered more than certainty.

"Count me," Zane said at her left. He stood close without touching. His nearness felt like a wall she trusted. "On three."

They did not reach three.

"South weft," Joren said to the room. His voice ran thin but straight. "Clinic vans at the old pumps. Drones in pairs. They adapt to flow." He swallowed. "They are learning us."

"Then we move faster than a lesson," Mireya said. "Rotate the uplink. Add dead pulses." She tapped the map and the lattice answered as a body that knew the hand.

They took the corridor toward the generator chamber. Concrete sweated. Wires sang a pitch between panic and peace. Zane walked a half step ahead, then let her pass pinch points first so he could slide through last and see what followed. Not manners. Math with feeling.

"Say it," Elia said when the tunnel narrowed. There was only room for breath and truths. "Whatever you are holding."

He did not slow. "At first," he said. He placed each word. "It was the tape."

Her chest tightened. A hand turned a hidden valve. She kept moving. "At first, I would have run if you had said that."

"And now?"

"Now we are under a city that wants us gone," she said. "Ask me later."

He nodded as if accepting a currency that might be worthless by morning. He did not apologize. He counted a breath at the next bend in a way that helped her feet. When she slid on condensate, he caught her elbow and let go before the touch could become a claim.

The generator chamber rose like a ribcage. Tall metal. The relay hummed and turned her teeth to instruments. Across the wall a small projection survived. A lullaby. A name. A laugh.

Elia faltered. The sight landed with a weight she could not put down.

"We cannot hold this room," Zane said. His breath cut her cheek. "They will bury us alive."

Mireya's voice cracked over the lowline. "Contact north and west. Hunters with boots."

Boots first. The opposite wall coughed stone. A hole opened white and mean. Enforcers poured through with mirrored visors. Drones dropped like punctuation. Red pupils tasted heat.

"Left bulkhead," Mireya shouted. She fired twice. An Enforcer fell and twitched and stilled. Joren flung a polished dish that was not a dish. A drone screamed and pinwheeled into a rack.

The boy clung to Elia's sleeve. Narrow shoulders. A mean shine at his pulse.

The counter-phrase slid in under the noise.

HARMONY IS HOME.
HOME IS QUIET.
QUIET IS CARE.

Elia did not argue. She opened her mouth and let her mother's words come through.

They rewrote your story. They renamed your hope.

The nearest drone stuttered. Zane moved into that stutter. He drove at the line. He did not shout. He did not need to. He was the largest moving answer in the room.

Bolts chewed metal where he had been. He went low and clean and slid his knife under a visor plate. The body hit hard and skittered. Heat scorched his shoulder open. He did not look. The cost had already been paid.

Elia pulled the boy toward the side exit. Joren stumbled into her peripheral with breath sawn thin. The slate was gone. He slapped a jammer onto a conduit. The room's hum hiccupped midword.

"Keep the signal," Mireya yelled. "Save the people."

An Enforcer pivoted toward Elia. Zane reached him first and took the line of fire as if he had done it many times. "Go," he mouthed through smoke.

Elia's throat tore itself into a sound she did not hear. Sirens and metal ate everything else. She dragged the boy. Joren shoved her shoulder and bought a yard. The side door bit and then let go. Cooler air waited. It carried a faint memory of outside.

She wanted to run without looking back. The world did not allow that mercy. She turned once. Zane's face carried blood at the lip and the color of a decision in his eyes.

"I was sent for the tape," he had said.

"I stayed for you," he had not had time to finish.

A drone shouldered through smoke. The lens dilated. It found Zane and locked. He did not blink. He shoved an

Enforcer into the beam. The man folded like a curtain that finally understood falling. Zane's knife found another seam.

The Union spoke in the forgiving tone it uses when it cuts and calls it care.

Sector 19. Commence purge.

The far wall split to a white that was not daylight. More Enforcers came. The chamber turned into a mouth full of teeth.

"Fall back," Mireya said. Steel under the break. "Save the signal."

Joren gripped the boy's arm. Elia gripped Joren's jacket. They moved as a single braced animal through the side throat. The floor heaved. A rack tore loose and fell like a sentence.

"Go," Zane shouted. Her feet obeyed.

An Enforcer lunged. Zane caught the rifle barrel with his bare hand and shoved it aside. He drove his knife up. Metal grated through a place not meant to be pierced. The body dropped. He kicked it free and turned to meet the next wave.

"Elia, run."

Her chest cinched. Rage and hurt twisted into a rope she threw forward as motion. The tunnel buckled under a new shock. Dust and heat swallowed the doorway with a savage kindness.

Mireya's rifle cracked twice.

"Not yet. Not yet. Now." Joren hauled. The boy sobbed into Elia's sleeve and held on. They reached the elbow of the exit and the wall admitted them with a shudder.

She looked back once. Refusing to look felt like its own betrayal. Zane drove his blade through an Enforcer's plate and pulled it free in a spit of sparks. He turned to the next. His shoulder ran dark. His chest heaved. His eyes found hers through the smoke, a wire pulled tight.

The tunnel tore.
Dust and fire swallowed him whole.

CHAPTER 13

RECALIBRATED

Smoke closed over the chamber and turned the air to chalk. Red wash strobed across broken conduit and the curled edges of a shredded map. Elia coughed grit from her throat, pressed a palm to the floor, and found her feet. Heat licked her cheek. The ceiling had blown a jagged mouth above the generators.

"Zane!" Her voice scraped.

A shape rose in the haze near the toppled console. He pushed a metal brace away, staggered once, and steadied. His cheek carried a split line. Blood darkened the shoulder seam of his jacket. He saw her and nodded, a tight flick that said still here.

"Report," Mireya called from the doorway. She moved along the wall, eyes on the ceiling, rifle ready.

"North seal gone," Joren answered, breath thin. He planted both hands on a panel and fed power back into the emergency string. Lights steadied to a hard orange.

A rumble rolled under their boots. Dust fell in a curtain. The city above them had begun pretending to be calm again; the station felt the lie.

Elia stepped into the hub. The city map hovered over the table, Sector lines clean, red pulses scattered like fresh wounds. Her throat dried. Those marks weren't little victories. They were doors the machine could now see.

"300,000 Bands burned through," Joren said. His thumb shook over the overlay. "Maybe more."

"We hold what we woke," Mireya said.

Elia touched the map rim to steady herself. "They will push back through language first."

"They already did," Zane said. He wiped blood from his mouth with the back of a hand. "Counsel scripts shifted tone. Kiosks started whispering correction."

"How do you know that?" Joren asked.

"Because I walked past one to get here and it told me to breathe through my grief." Zane looked at Elia. "Sound doesn't unring."

A runner slid through the door with a slate clutched in both hands. "Sector 4 nurses locked the MedCenter. People in gowns are holding hands with nurses. They jammed doors with carts."

The comms cracked: "Kade on grid—Sector 9 lights are long. Window thirty. You're clear if you move now."

Mireya let one breath show. "Good."

A cold rip crossed the room. Joren's pupils tightened into thin chips of black. His hand drifted toward an access panel as if pulled.

"Joren." Mireya's voice landed like a thrown stone.

"We should open the north tunnel," he said in a voice that belonged to no one in the room. Calm. Helpful. "Invite them in. Negotiate a reset. Comply."

Elia moved. She caught his wrist before his fingers reached the panel and slammed it into the steel. Pain reached him where her words could not. The calm glazed look cracked. His mouth opened on a gasp.

"Pulse," the medic barked.

Elia tore a lead off a dead Band, bit the copper clean, and pressed it to Joren's cuff. The shock snapped him back. He retched, wiped his mouth with the back of his hand, and looked at her with his own eyes again.

"I'm here," he said.

"Stay with me," Mireya told him, softer than steel.

Elia's wrist flared where the Band had burned her. A voice rose in her head the way chill rises from a stairwell: *you're tired, sweetheart, let someone else steer.* She closed her fist until the ache steadied her.

"We move before they finish their recalibration," she said. "We go at the memory root."

"The Archives," Mireya answered, already with her. "You know a door?"

Elia held the map in her mind. "South Gate river intake. The coolant line runs past an old maintenance hall. Welded grate, not sealed. I can cut without losing the wall."

"Gel," Mireya said. She pushed a foil packet and a coil of line into Elia's hands. "It will howl. Ride it. If you see your mother in there, do nothing she asks unless she bleeds when you cut."

Elia nodded once.

Zane shifted closer. His voice kept the noise out. "Ward, once you're in, look for the older spindle. It still takes a hand."

She met his eyes. "Why do you know where my hands belong?"

He almost answered. Something moved in his face and then locked. "Because I watched you work through glass once and the machine didn't like how fast you learn."

She nearly said I know you and bit the words back. The station did not need another thing to hear.

"Positions," Mireya said. "We buy her room to breathe."

"I'll ride the board," Kade said from the console, fingers on the old relay. "If the kiosk tone shifts, I'll call the turn."

The hub spun into motion. Harness buckles clicked. Boots hit stone with intent. Elia looped the coil to her belt and slid the gel into her pocket.

Zane fell in beside her as they entered the maintenance hall. The tunnel sloped. Water sweat stained the pipe bellies. Metal smelled of rain without a sky to give it.

"You still trust me?" he asked.

"I trust the work," she said.

"That wasn't the question."

She didn't look at him. "You almost answered something that mattered and stopped." She stepped around a fallen brace. "That was my answer."

He let that sit. At the bend where the wall carried a smear of grease that read as a prayer, he touched her sleeve with two fingers. "Count three, then cut."

She pocketed the need to ask what he had been about to say. It burned there. It kept her moving.

They reached the grate by smell. Old iron. River cold.

Elia smeared gel around the lattice seam. The packet warmed in her fingers. She struck the little flint. The ring of gel flashed, then burned with a white drip that bit the welds. The grate screamed. The sound convinced her teeth they were part of the wall. Welds gave like gristle. Water breathed out through the opening and turned her shins to ice.

"Go," Zane said.

"Hold the line," she told him.

"I will."

She pulled the grate and slid into the river throat. Cold climbed fast. Stone scraped a line down her shoulder. Current tried to lay her flat and make choices for her. She rolled a shoulder into the push and found the bottom with her palms. The rope paid out behind her; two hard tugs came back: I'm here.

She counted her strokes because numbers do not lie when air runs short. The tunnel bent left. She went left. Bars kissed her ribs and then let her through. A sump took her and threw her into black air that tasted like old rain and copper.

She clung to a furred ladder, found rungs, climbed. A hatch gave under her weight and let her into a corridor that hummed for no one. Lights buzzed. A cleaning drone dozed in its dock.

She listened. No boots yet. No voice yet. The Archive air carried cold that had never seen winter.

She moved left, then left again where the cold strengthened. The hall opened into a room with racks for walls and glass for ribs. Lights blinked in patient colors. Her skin prickled.

"Ward," a voice said from the ceiling. Measured. Kind in the way of razors. "Well done."

Carrow did not need a face to be present. The room carried him.

"Where did my mother sing the lullaby?" Elia asked. She kept her tone bored, the way a clerk asks for a form.

"In a kitchen with a single narrow window," he answered at once. "Light on tile, steam on glass."

"What did she smell like after rain?"

"Cardamom," he said, "and rust."

Her jaw set. "You always add rust."

"It suits," he said.

"For you."

She stepped past the first rack without touching anything. A panel near the floor gave when she leaned her shoulder into it. Behind it, a crawl. She slid inside and pulled the panel back. The air cooled another degree. The spindle would stand two chambers beyond, where an old relay waited for hands.

"Ward," Carrow said. His voice softened. "The chair saved your city from eating itself. You know this. You were the one who—"

She killed the feed. The hum returned. No more voice. Not yet.

The crawl narrowed. Her shoulder scraped something sharp and sent heat across her skin. She breathed through it and reached the spindle column. A seam of copper ran down its side. She set the burned oval of her wrist against it.

The scar heated under the contact. The metal woke with a quiet lick of light. She could almost feel the recognition move. Not magic. A cheap biometric that should never have survived a consolidation. She turned the manual release with careful pressure.

Air shifted behind her. Wet fabric whispered against metal. Boots, light on their edges. The patrol moved well. Zane dropped into the crawl, rolled onto a hip, and braced a hand over her head to shield her from the panel's corner.

"Don't touch the release," he said. His voice came ragged and close. "They keyed it to her voice."

"Whose?"

"The Architect," he said. "It will sing recall in your bones."

A visor slid into view at floor level just outside the crawl. Red light cut a coin across the seam. Another followed. The rack trembled as a rifle nose set against it.

Zane lifted a piece of snapped heatsink from the darkness, flicked it low across the open floor. It clattered to their left. A bolt chased the noise and bit into steel. Sparks sprayed.

"Two more," he breathed. His forearm shook over her head. He studied the flick of red on the panel seam to feel their timing.

"Zane," she whispered.

He shifted just enough to hear her. The closeness made space feel scarce.

"You were coming to tell me something," she said. "Before the crawl."

His eyes did not leave the seam. "Yes."

"What?"

He exhaled once. "I knew you before all this, and I am afraid I will say it wrong."

A bolt hissed past the crawl mouth and ate a strip off the panel. The metal glowed, then dimmed. The first visor dipped for a better angle.

Zane counted under his breath. "One. Two." He leaned close, mouth at her ear. "Run."

◄◄ ► ▐▌ ■ ►►

The city put its costume back on. Server farms woke in rows. Rails returned to green. Drones drifted in calm patterns and wrote quiet circles in the air. A billboard above District 12 poured glossy water into a glass that would never sweat. People watched themselves in the reflection and tried to match the picture.

On the street below, Reya strung two halves of a burned Band around her neck and held a loaf under her arm. She stood on a crate and looked left, then right. Neighbors who never chose sides came because standing still had begun to feel like choosing wrong.

"You are not broken," she told them. Her voice shook on the first word and steadied on the rest. "You were lied to."

Someone laughed without humor. Someone else cried. A child took the crust she offered and did not look at the drones that dropped through the glare and hung at head height. Their lenses blinked, recording with gentle interest. They did not fire. Yet.

In Sector 4, nurses slid crash carts into lifts and taped doors. A woman in a paper gown folded another woman's fingers into hers. A little plastic speaker that once told people when to breathe began to play a field recording of wind in tall grass. No one asked who had loaded it. The room gained height.

High in the Core Tower, Director Aric watched the feeds steady themselves. The Protocol Architect stood at his shoulder, visor silver, voice precise. Carrow waited one pace back, hands folded as if in prayer he did not believe in.

"Soft cleanse queued," the Architect said. "Baseline affect returns within six hours."

"Begin," Aric said.

Carrow stepped closer to the glass. "Subject Elia Ward," he said. "Classification: contagion of thought." He didn't raise his voice. He didn't have to.

Technicians set parameters. Meditation kiosks added a colder ninth note. Counsel prompts folded in a new phrase: **RECALL DIRECTIVE.**

The first wave of sleepers blinked and wondered why tears had warmed their faces. The room logged everything and asked for more.

Carrow watched a fragment of an old clip slide across a side screen: a woman turning, not quite smiling; a child with a Band that slipped on a thin wrist. He set two fingers to the screen's edge. "Observe," he said. "She will choose the door that hurts."

◄◄ ► ❙❙ ■ ►►

Water beat a steady drum behind Elia's ribs. The rack shook again as a boot hit steel. Zane tucked her deeper under the overhang of conduit and laid his palm flat above her to take the next impact. The red coin of the visor searched the seam, slid on, returned.

Elia set her mouth near his ear. "If they keyed the release, how do we open it?"

"We don't," he said. "We bypass."

"Show me."

He lifted his hand an inch, found her wrist by feel, and placed her fingers on a narrow line of copper that ran away from the seam into the shadow of the housing. "Here," he said. "This is older than the key. It wants pressure and heat, nothing clever."

His voice had dropped into the tone he used when he taught a lock. Calm. Exact. She matched that tone. The fear steadied.

"On three," he said again, but now he counted the bolts. A shot cracked to their right. A breath. Another to their left. He nodded. "Now."

She pressed her scar to the copper and held. Heat climbed into her skin in a slow burn. The metal clicked once, twice. A relay on the far side engaged with a tired snick.

The first soldier crouched and shoved his rifle under the rack. Zane caught the barrel, shoved it sideways, and drove his knife into the soft joint between plate and glove. The body folded. The second fired blind. Sparks chewed the rack above their heads.

"Go," Zane said, and he pushed her through the gap in a single smooth shove that sent her into the dark beyond the spindle.

She landed hard on a grate, rolled, and came up on a knee with the knife in her hand. The room opened in front of her in tall aisles of glass and cable. Cold air moved across her face. Somewhere a speaker clicked to life and died, as if unsure who should be speaking now.

Behind her, Zane slid out of the crawl, shoulder first, teeth clenched. He looked over his left forearm at the patrol he had just made hesitate. A streak of blood ran under his collar. He didn't notice.

He turned to her. Whatever he had almost said lived in his eyes.

"Later," she said. "We finish the work."

He nodded once.

Boots hammered at their backs. The visor coins found them again. Elia ran.

She ran because the city had learned to pretend and people had not, because sound that rings does not forget itself, because the machine preferred keys to knives and she had decided to be both. She took the left aisle.

Zane came at her shoulder, breath tight, steps exact. The patrol closed. A bolt tore a channel down the edge of a glass spine and filled the air with a bright chemical smell.

The old spindle stood ahead with its face turned slightly away, as if shy. Copper glinted under a braid of cable. Elia reached for it. Zane turned his head, listened to the feet behind them, and leaned close.

"Run."

CHAPTER 14
PERIPHERAL GHOSTS

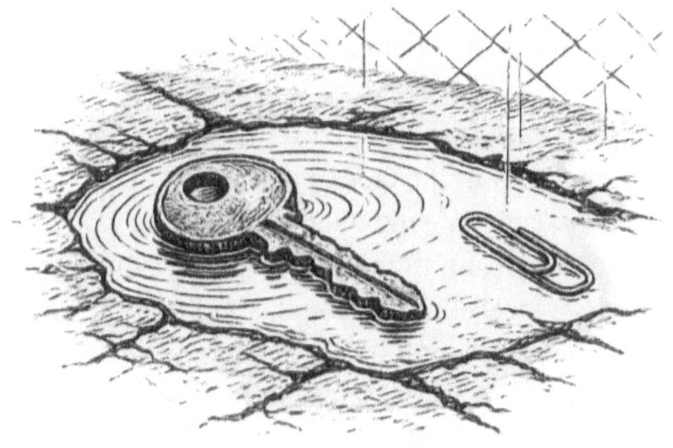

Zane twisted, drew the patrol's eyes with a scrape of metal, and sent a shard skittering hard right. Bolts chased the noise. Elia slid left, shoulder tight to the rack, palm on cold conduit. She felt the spindle's face at her back, the click she had woken with heat and pressure. The visor coin returned, searching. Zane hooked a boot behind a fallen shelf and heaved. Glass ribs toppled in a bright rush. The aisle filled with broken light. Shouts. One clean opening.

They went.

A low hatch gave to a service shaft. Zane dropped first. Elia followed, ribs brushing steel, boots finding ladder rungs by guess and habit. Air smelled of coolant and old rain. They hit a sump, waded, turned once where the current bent, and climbed through a grate into a dark that hummed like a buried heart. The station took them back as if it had expected them.

Mireya met them at the bend. "Alive," she said. She looked them both in the face to confirm it. "Good. The Core is listening harder. We move on the Rim."

"Copy," Kade said in their ears. "Rim scanners polling wrists before faces. I'm seeding dead tags along Sector 9."

Joren shoved a small tin at Elia. Inside lay a cuff no heavier than a coin. Matte shell. Scuffed. Dead. "Wear it," he said. "Rim scanners look at wrists before faces."

"I am not putting a leash back on," Elia said.

"It is a costume," Joren answered. "It fools the first glance. It carries a spoof tag so cheap the scanners stop caring. If they want to look closer, we are already in trouble."

She held the cuff. The oval of burn on her wrist prickled. Zane watched her without pushing. He had blood in his hair and dust along his jaw. He looked like a man who had run out of lies to tell himself.

"Fine," she said. She snapped the cuff over the scar. The dead shell sat light and hateful. Joren stuck a thin thermal square under the housing. "Passive patch," he said. "Warms when skin temp shifts. It reads as calm in a crowd."

"And near him?" she asked before she could decide not to.

Joren blinked once, surprised, then not. "He runs a tight jammer. It steadies everything in his bubble. The patch will reflect that."

Zane said nothing. He only looked at the cuff with a face that knew the cost of wearing one and the cost of not.

They ate what passed for food and took three minutes on pallet and crate. Elia set her shoulder to the wall and let her eyes shut without permission. Sleep rose at a run.

In the dream she stood at a window she could not name. Rain misted the glass. On the other side, a man leaned his forearms on a sill and laughed low in his throat at something only she heard. Same mouth. Same jaw. Same heat at the corner of his eyes when he turned. She reached for the pane. Cold touched her palm. The image trembled and brightened. He looked up. Zane. She woke with her hand flat on the wall.

"Ready?" Mireya asked.

"Yes." Elia found her feet. The cuff sat wrong and she refused to adjust it.

◄◄ ► ❚❚ ■ ►►

"Two stops. Drop left door. Camera blind for six." Kade said.

They took the rim tram where the city frayed. The car rode with a tired sway. The towers thinned. Lights turned from gloss to glare. Block edges rose crooked. Rain traced silver on cracked screens and ran down into gutters that smelled of solder and algae. People kept their heads low. The Union had not bothered to feather this edge with calm.

Zane stood in the car's doorway with one hand on the bar and one on the knife he kept low. He watched rooflines and the gaps under stairs. When the tram sighed to a stop he stepped first to test the ground. The cuff on Elia's wrist warmed as he came close. Not hot. Just a quiet settle, as if the skin had remembered a signal and leaned toward it.

"Sector 9," he said. The words carried history. "Nothing dies out here. It forgets what it was told to be."

"Does that help us?" she asked.

"It helps me stay careful."

They moved off the line and into streets that had learned to sag. A store with wire for glass hunched in on itself at the corner. A man on a crate watched the rain. His Band had been smashed long ago and left to heal into his wrist. Two fingers were gone from his right hand. He noted their faces with slow interest.

"Not from here," he said. He did not smile. "Not hiding either."

Zane's thumb slid along the sheath at his belt. Elia kept walking. The man flicked a chipped key into a puddle near her boot.

"Ping if the key's bait," Kade said. "I'll spike a siren three blocks over."

"Down the hatch," he said. "Two ladders. Follow the stink. Take the left when the right looks safer. If the lights turn red, crawl."

"You sell people?" Zane asked.

"If I wanted you sold," the man said, "I would have said your names already." He lifted his eyes to Elia. They were young inside a ruined face. "We remember now."

The words landed under her ribs and stayed. She bent and picked up the key. Zane shook his head. She met the look and kept the key anyway.

"If he is bait?" Zane asked as they rounded the corner.

"Then we fight."

Something eased in his mouth. Not a smile. Not that far from one. He lifted the hatch. Rust sighed. Air rose from below with the weight of old damp. He tested the first rung. It held. He went down and she followed, palms blackened, breath steady by choice.

◄◄ ► ❙❙ ■ ►►

The shadow grid did not pretend to be a place for people. Wires hung wet. Mold furred the edges of panels where leaks had lived too long. A small maintenance bot knelt dead with its head to the wall as if ashamed. White threads grew through its speaker grill. Zane named what would cut, what would slip, what would bite. She leaned to hear and that closeness pulled other memories forward, the crawlspace and his forearm braced over her, his mouth at her ear, the way her body had matched his count before her mind caught up.

"Why did you stay?" she asked. She meant the field and the fight and the wall he made of himself when the room filled with bolts.

"When?" he asked, making her say it straight.

"In the chamber. You had a window."

"You have the fragment," he said.

"So math."

"Survival," he said.

The word sat under her skin with edges. "And now?"

"Now it is still survival," he said.

She breathed once through the feeling. The corridor opened to a junction where a small panel still glowed, the

161

last coal in a grate. Mireya's map had called it a blind relay, a thing the Union had forgotten to count because no one had reminded it to be afraid of this corner in years.

"Quick work," Zane said. "The longer we stand, the smarter the city gets."

Joren's voice came light in Elia's ear. "Scanners up ahead read pulses, not faces. Your cuffs will pass if you are boring. Do not be interesting."

Elia took the fragment from its sealed cloth and felt it warm along her palm. Recognition ran up the tendons like current. Breath in. Hands first. Thinking later. That order had kept her alive.

A thin whine drew tight behind them. Zane's hand rode her shoulder once, a touch that said still with me. A tall figure stepped into the corridor, movements too quiet for a space this small.

"Step away from the node," the voice said. Male and not. Human-shaped and smoothed until nothing true could catch on it.

The man's face was glass with features written under it like a sketch. The line at his jaw cut wrong, as if a mouth had been added and taken away. No Band. No nameplate. Only a small logo embossed at the throat. Theta.

"Elia Ward," he said. "You are a threat to harmonic order."

Zane moved first. Knife low. Elia slid left and fed the fragment into the port. It took with a click that felt in bone. The node woke. Transmission leaped outward like a bird hitting glass.

Theta's spine brightened. Orange. Red. Black. His head twitched as if distant hands had seized the nerves. He lunged anyway because that was what he was made to do. Zane yanked Elia clear before a pipe slammed the floor where her knee had been. The sound wrote itself in her jaw.

She crouched and steadied the recorder. The readout stuttered, then held. Patterns lived in the stall points. Not luck. Not a ghost glitch. The machine was learning and so were they.

Up on the Rim, old signs flickered awake. In rooms where sockets had been covered, dead screens blinked once and made faces from static. Not real. Not human. Mouth. Eyes. A suggestion of a voice. A single word rose thin and steady. *Remember.*

Elia heard her own cadence inside it. The set of her teeth on the last syllable. The breath before. A small tilt she had never named. The recognition scraped her skin. She forced air into her chest and looked away from what she knew.

Theta's eyes flashed a wrong blue. He turned. He ran. Not at them. Away. The end of the corridor took him. Water forgot him.

Silence lowered. Dust hung in the lightless air. A sweet coolant note lay on her tongue from a cracked line. Elia pried the fragment free. It almost slipped. Zane's fingers closed on her wrist long enough to pin the tremor. The cuff warmed under his touch. She felt heat move and realized the thermal square had its own small language. Near him, the dead shell settled. The status dot softened. A lie that looked like calm.

"You should have left me," she said.

"Could not," he said.

She turned. His hand slid along her inner wrist as he let go. Heat followed the path. The corridor was a narrow world—damp wire, concrete, his breath close. The small hairs along his jaw caught light darker than the rest. Blood drew a line at his temple. He raised his other hand, slow, not to make her flinch and not to test his own. His fingers touched the angle of her jaw and left a new temperature behind.

"Stop looking at me like that," she said.

"Like what?" he asked.

"Like you already decided," she said.

Something worked in his jaw and stilled. "Maybe I did."

Her spine found the wall. The city still threw ghosts against dead glass, but down here the only things that counted were the wet drum behind her ribs and his measured breath and the way the cuff warmed when he leaned in. He bent only so far. His voice rasped heat. "Tell me no."

Her mouth remembered the word the city had learned. Her ribs remembered another word. She chose. "No," she said, and meant do not stop.

He swore quiet. His hand on her wrist tightened and drew her a fraction closer as he came that same fraction. His mouth found hers, not to take but to meet. Knees softened. She caught his jacket, felt hard muscle under wet cloth, and the hitch in his breath when she did. Old wire hummed. Water counted time.

A dry click opened near her ear. Zane's head turned. He pulled her flat and lifted the knife. A hair-thin red line crept along a pipe seam. A drone had found a hole. "We are not alone," he said. His blade flicked. Metal sang. The light died. Above, something small hit concrete and did not hit again.

He rested his forehead against hers for one breath. "We finish this upstairs," he said. He made the thin phrase into a promise, not an escape. "Now we move."

"Two minutes," she said. The words shook. She did not care.

"Two minutes," he agreed.

He kissed her once more. Not an argument. A reason. She let the city hear the sound it pulled from her and did not apologize. The wires carried it where they always carry what people will not say out loud.

They moved.

◄◄ ► ❙❙ ■ ►►

The hatch key from the man on the crate opened a rusted square two blocks deeper into the Rim. Below lay a maintenance throat pointed south. The air smelled of river damp and old batteries. Zane went first, boots finding bolts instead of plates. Elia followed, count steady, breath quiet. Her cuff stayed warm in his wake. In a wider cavity they paused. Joren's voice threaded in. "Watch your pairing. The grid has started flagging pairs that move in a pattern. If you can, trade lead."

Zane stepped back. "You first."

She took point. The cuff cooled as the space between them grew. She looked down at it and hated the logic. She waited at the bend and let him close until the warmth returned.

"You see it too?" she asked.

His eyes flicked to the dot, then to her face. "I do."

"What does it mean?"

"That the machine reads better than it used to," he said. "Or that we built this lie too well."

"Or both," she said.

They reached the blind relay under the old water works, a box the size of a suitcase wedged behind a corroded panel. Zane pried the cover. Elia slid the recorder's lead into a port with corroded edges. The map on her slate brightened. A chain of cold rooms appeared under a block of government offices to the east. One marked brighter. *Sanctum.* The core archive. The place the city kept for erasing what did not serve it.

The relay spit a string of labels. Gate. Voice. Clearance. A name appeared and vanished, censored by the machine's own fear.

"Can you pull the key?" Zane asked.

"Not the key," she said. "The lock's signature. Enough to know whose mouth opens it."

She ran the trace. The audio schema unfolded in a tight braid. Tone. Formant. Breathing curve. A model signature appeared:

ARCH-PRIME

Under it, a smaller tag flickered.

I. Ward

Crossed out. Replaced. The machine had scratched her mother's name out of its own memory and written something colder.

Zane read the header and went very still. "They keyed the Sanctum to her voice," he said. "Not your mother. The Architect."

Elia stared at the line until it steadied. She had believed the door wanted her bloodline. That had felt cruel and almost bearable. This felt worse. It meant the city trusted only the mouth that taught it how to forget.

"We have to get a slice of her voice," she said. "Or teach the lock to accept a cousin."

Zane tapped the thermal patch on her cuff with a knuckle. "We have one lever," he said. "You carry a line the machine keeps bending toward. We might make it believe you are close enough."

"Or we borrow something," Joren said in her ear, voice tight with held breath. "The public clinics run counsel scripts in her tone. Crude copies, but copies."

Mireya cut in. "No more talk. Move. Patrols rerouted on the Rim. They adapted. They are following your pair pattern."

The corridor ahead brightened at the edges, not with light but with attention. A drone nose came through a seam, lens slit widening. Another followed. They learned. They came quiet.

Zane slid a heatsink square along the floor. It clattered against a wall and fell. The drones tracked sound out of habit. Habit failed them when Elia was already moving. Bait. Misdirect. Escape. Zane's hand found her shoulder long enough to steer the second turn. The cuff warmed. The lens missed. They cut left through a narrow throat where pipes ate the light.

A figure stood at the exit like a shadow that had changed its mind about being a shadow. Agent Theta. He looked at Elia and then at Zane. Something behind the glass tried to solve a problem and did not like the answer. The jaw seam flexed.

"Subject pair," he said. "Proximity breach."

"Come get us," Zane said, and stepped into him.

No long fight. No list of moves. One clean hit to the knee joint where synthetic met hinge, one twist that took the elbow, one shove that put a heavy body into a wall of wet conduit. Sparking water bit the casing. Theta's lights flickered. He reset like a machine that could not admit the error.

Elia threw the last of the cutting gel at the corner seam and lit it. The flare screamed. The drones flinched. Sound lived in metal again, not code. She felt the passage open behind the noise. Zane felt it too.

"Now," he said.

They ran. Stairs climbed. Water winded. The Rim accepted them back in a spit of gray rain.

They cut through a market lane that smelled of oil and flatbread and solder. Faces looked up and looked away. A boy tapped three fingers against his throat and a woman shook her head no and pulled him close. Two Memory Clinic vans idled at the far end with engines that sounded kind. A nurse stood in a doorway and did not meet anyone's eyes. A drone tracked the street with patient hunger.

Elia and Zane kept moving. They did not touch. The cuff warmed anyway. A scanner over a shop door glanced at their wrists and lost interest. The lie held long enough to matter.

"My dreams keep awakening my past."

At the tram pylons Zane slowed, only a step. "Do you recognize someone," he asked. "in the dream?"

"Yes."

"Me?"

She looked at his mouth, his jaw, the small heat at the corner of his eyes when he looked up. The same as the window. The same as before she knew the name of that window. "Yes."

"Then the machine did not take everything."

"Or it left bait," she said. "For me."

"Either way," he said, "we use it."

The tram shuddered and pulled in. People climbed on with heads down. A Clinic van turned the corner slow, lights calm, speakers murmuring.

HARMONY IS HOME

HOME IS QUIET

QUIET IS CARE.

Elia looked at the slate one more time.

ARCH-PRIME

Glowed in small hard letters. The lock wanted the Architect. The city's deepest door would open only to the voice that had taught it how to close.

"We go after her," she said.

Zane nodded. The cuff warmed again. The tram doors slid shut. The Rim blurred to rain. The city watched. The next plan started to breathe.

CHAPTER 15
ARCHITECT'S KEY

Two minutes was a promise and a dare and a clock with a blade. Zane's mouth found hers again, not careful now. His hand framed her jaw, thumb warm under her ear. Concrete pressed cold through her coat and made his heat burn brighter.

"Tell me no," he breathed.

"Don't you dare stop," she said, and the last of her carefulness cracked.

Water ticked from a seam. The floor slicked her soles. A relay hummed like a gnat near the edge of hearing. He braced one forearm beside her head, not a trap, a shelter, and drew her that last inch. She hooked his jacket and pulled. Fabric gave a tired sound. His laugh broke and vanished into the next kiss.

His ribs worked hard under her palms. When she flattened her hand to his chest he covered it, pressing, as if to say keep this. She rose onto her toes and his restraint went to pieces. Rain and copper lived in his mouth. She gave him her answer. No speech. Only the sound a body makes when it remembers it is allowed to want.

The node's hum ran fine along her skin. His hand slid to her waist, slow enough to be checked. She nodded because words would have wrecked her. The space between wanting and knowing you are wanted closed fast enough to steal breath. When he bent to her throat and marked her once, she let her head touch the wall and did not hide the sound that rose. He swallowed it like a thank you.

His comm ticked, a polite digital cough that had no place here. He killed it blind, knuckles rapping plastic, never leaving her mouth. She smiled into the kiss, mean and delighted. He felt it and laughed again, that shredded little sound that should not have lived in a corridor like this and did. Inside the urgency he still kept her safe. His palm sat behind her head where a pipe waited. His shoulders turned to take corners if the corridor bit. She met him with the same care. When he broke for air she chased him rather than let the cold in.

"Tell me when," he said against her cheek.

She did. Not with numbers. With a grip and a gasp and the way every muscle said now.

After, she let her forehead rest against his for one slow breath and then the world came back in pieces. Hum. Water. A faint metallic buzz above, something shifting. Not fear in her legs, just tremor. He kept his hand at her hip as if the air might not hold her yet. He kissed the corner of her mouth like an apology to all the rules that had told him not to want. Something under her breastbone rearranged into a shape that could hold warmth without spilling.

"Zane," she said. He went still. "Earlier, when the broadcast hit, did you hear it?"

"I heard it."

"The way it sounded?"

He waited.

"It sounded like me."

She had not meant to say that. It came out anyway. His breath changed. He did not tell her she was wrong. He did not tell her she was right. He looked like a man with answers he had kept in a pocket so long they were warm to the touch.

He lifted her hand and kissed her knuckles instead. "Two minutes are gone," he said. "We move."

She nodded. The clock insisted. She tugged her coat straight. The decoy Band lay dead on her wrist. As he shifted past her in the pinch of the corridor it warmed once, small and traitorous. She noted it and said nothing.

The pressure changed every ten steps on the way out, the air tightening and relaxing like breath. "Patrol path," he said, counting under his breath. The sweep tightened exactly when skin met skin, as if the city kept score on touch. A Clinic repeater hid behind a cracked grate. He lifted the faceplate with two fingers. She clipped a lead, fed the mic, and took three seconds of top-line prompt. The voice came thin and clipped. The cadence rang clean where it mattered.

"Got it," she said.

He dropped the faceplate, and they were moving before the echo settled. At the last ladder she climbed first and he came last, a habit he could not drop. Rain found them when she hauled the hatch. Sector 9 gave back the crooked skyline and plastic bandages on windows, the diesel breath of generators patching around holes she had cut in the grid.

The safehouse smelled like metal fatigue and human worry. She knelt on cracked tile and wrapped the fragment in gauze that clung like a held breath. She lifted the mat, slid the packet under the false panel in the concrete, and let her fingers hover there for a beat, the way you do when trust feels like a weight you could leave behind if you wanted to be lighter and you do not want to be lighter anymore.

Mireya watched from the door without putting a question in her mouth. She tightened the magnetic netting and spoke to the room. "That transmission hit more than local. Upper-sector receivers lit. People are asking."

"Curiosity without guidance gets crushed," Zane said from the wall.

"We guide them," Elia said before Mireya could answer.

Joren had a scope wired to a battered slate. He ran the capture and winced. "Dirty," he said. "But the shape holds. Seventy-eight percent match to executive prompts."

"Seventy-eight holds across three nodes," Kade said from the bench, eyes on the scope. "Dirty shape, true bone."

She heard the rise before the word and knew it like a scar. She felt her own mouth copy the small breath the voice took on the second beat. "Show me the curve."

Joren threw the wave on the plaster. It wasn't pretty. It was true where it mattered. She traced the notch with a nail. "They key Sanctum with this?"

"Her variants sit on top," Joren said. "Architect's voice wraps the bone. This is the bone."

Mireya cut three automatic processes from the terminal and killed the room's nervous habits. The old projectors threw maps and dust on the wall, red pencil lines, hand-written frequencies, exit arrows like veins out of a beating thing. "Old routes only," she said. "No grid. No Bands. If they want to find us, they walk."

Zane pushed off the wall and came nearer. "You want to fake the key?" he said to Elia.

"I want to teach the lock a different song," she said. "Not today. Soon."

"You think you can carry her register?"

Elia closed her eyes and let the streets run across her tongue. She lifted her chin and gave three syllables to the stale air.

Joren's slate ticked. "Close," he said. "Too honest at the end."

"Keep working it," Mireya said. "Not on the net."

Mireya dragged a little tone box from a drawer and set it down. The speaker hissed and settled. She rolled the dial until a thin line of sound stood straight on the tiny glass. "She hides a skip," Mireya said. "Regular, then a cut."

"I'll ride the carrier low," Kade said. "If Prime flattens key, I nudge neutral."

Elia tried the word. "Remember."

The needle spiked, then wandered. Wrong.

Zane tilted his head, listening not to the speaker but to the place her breath started. "You rush the second beat," he said. "You always did."

"How would you know that?"

"You count on fours. You always did."

She tried again, softer. The needle steadied, then dipped late. Wrong again. She loosened her jaw, set her tongue where the Architect would, and refused to feel like a thief. Again. The box whined.

Mireya tapped the glass with a knuckle, coaxing a stubborn gauge.

Zane moved closer, not touching. He matched her breathing, quiet, so she could feel the rhythm against her shoulder. Four in. Four out. He did not lead. He gave her a wall to push against.

She set the shape in her mouth one more time. She cut the breath where the script would and then, at the last instant, softened the last consonant the way she did with children.

The needle stood straight. It wavered a hair, then chose to hold.

Mireya's eyes flicked to a side light that had not woken in months. It tried, failed, tried again. "Close," she said. "Close is enough to reach the door."

Zane watched Elia shape silence again. He kept one hand on the back of a chair he did not sit in. He spoke low, only for her. "You still count your breaths on fours when you're scared."

Her eyes opened. "How would you know that?"

He was quiet a second too long. "I watch," he said. True, but not the whole of it.

The door rattled once, a coded knock. Mireya cracked it an inch. A runner slid in, pressed his palm to his chest before speaking. "Sector 12. Bread lines turned into talk lines. Drones held. No fire. Names got said out loud."

Mireya's jaw loosened. "Reya?"

"On a crate," the runner said. "She said the line. The boy did too."

Elia felt the word rise under the floor like water finding a low spot. "Remember."

"Guide it," she told the runner. "No speeches. Quiet links. Pairs."

He nodded and slipped back out.

A boy in Sector 12 lay awake staring at his ceiling because his Band still flashed. He took it off, turned it in his hands, put it back on like he had been taught, then dragged a notebook from under his bed. He drew the girl he had seen between alerts and wrote the word once, small, along the margin. He said it under his breath and flinched at how his mouth wanted to say it in a rhythm that wasn't entirely his.

Far out where Pulse seldom reached, an old woman felt the wind change. She lifted her chin as if someone had knocked. She opened a cupboard and unwrapped a thin cloth bundle she had kept under the salt. A patch looked up with its stubborn kindness. "Remember." She set it on the table and laid a cup over it for now.

Zane stayed on Elia. "You don't want a crowd?"

"I don't want a stampede," she said. "They trained people to follow volume. We teach them to follow choice."

He took that. He looked like a man who could stand on ground that moved. The analog relay that had carried her signal flickered. Mireya slapped the casing and wired around the weakness in three neat moves. "You just painted targets on every node that ever housed us."

"I know," Elia said.

"They shaved minutes," Zane said. He did not need a clock to feel it. When old protocols wake you feel them through your feet. "Sanctum is live."

Elia's throat tightened, not fear, decision. "We move the board," she said to Mireya. "The prompt cadence is the wedge. We seed a variant where it hurts. Not noise. Memory. The kind you cannot sell back."

"Where?"

"The Archive spine."

Zane turned his head. "You mean to walk in with her key?"

"I mean to make the lock doubt itself," she said. "If it doubts, it opens where we choose or closes where they need it open."

Mireya watched her a long second. "This isn't bravado," she said. "It's craft. Good."

Elia let out air. Not relief. Alignment.

Zane leaned close again. "You still call storms library weather," he said.

The words hit like a hidden step. "How would you know that?"

"Because once you fell asleep on a floor of stacked books and said it in your sleep."

"When?"

Before he answered, the wall vent coughed twice, the pressure warning. Mireya jerked her chin at the corridor. "Later." Zane had already stepped back from the truth he had almost set down. He looked sick with it and kept moving.

◄◄ ► ❚❚ ■ ►►

Somewhere else, the city tried to impose a center. Screens poured alerts, then red banners that wanted to be

177

answers. Director Aric's boots struck obsidian like punctuation.

"This isn't a glitch," Commander Veren said. "It's a breach."

The Protocol Architect's visor held a thin silver curve where eyes should be. Her voice cut clean.

"Affect spikes correlate to proximity events. The subject's touch changes pursuit timing."

Aric flicked two fingers. A map filled with red bars that tightened and relaxed in a rhythm that looked like breath.

"Exploit it."

Carrow stood one pace back, the kind of face machines like.

A frame froze. Elia, mid-breath, dust on her cheek. Shadow behind. In the corner, one word burned: *Remember.*

"Enhance," Aric said, though no one needed it.

"She's marked," Veren muttered.

Carrow's fingers tightened on his tablet. Two thin veins stood along his knuckles. He let go.

"Sanctum is deprecated," he said, mild as tea.

"Deprecated is not dead," Aric answered.

"Reauthorize."

In the cooled belly of a building that pretended to be maintenance, locks learned Aric's palm and then his heat. Sanctum's hum deepened the way a chest does when a person takes breath to speak. He did not wait to hear it.

◄◄ ► ❚❚ ■ ►►

Back in the safehouse, Mireya shouldered a bag and cut power with a knife switch that had saved them longer than any code. Blueprints died. The hum sank. The only light left came from the thin pain of emergency LEDs, and then those winked out because living had become the art of not being seen. Air shifted. Close by, metal began to lower with patient confidence. The first sign was the wind it made, a cold tongue along stone.

"On your feet," Mireya said. "Bags. Masks. If you leave something, leave the thing you can miss."

Buckles clicked. Boots scuffed. Zane checked his knife. His fingers ghosted along Elia's wrist where he had held her. The decoy Band warmed again. The sweep time on her comm cut in half between one blink and the next.

"We don't have the minutes we had," he said.

"We never did," she said. Something fierce and grateful broke open in his face and closed into resolve.

"Let them listen," she said for the walls and the wire. "We'll teach them what to hear."

They moved. The tunnel breathed cold, then colder. Mireya killed telltale hums with a knuckle and pulled fuses the way some people pull weeds. Zane took corners with his weight where danger would break first. Elia chose angles the gate maps had never imagined. A lazy red beam crawled the pipe above. She flattened and pulled them through the dead space under it by their pack straps. Steel hissed behind and bit nothing.

A kiosk coughed the prompt in the Architect's cadence inside a wall they passed. The shard in her pocket answered like a struck wire. The decoy Band warmed in counterpoint.

"They're tracking proximity," Zane said.

"Good," she said. "Then they'll be wrong where we choose."

"Count me," he said.

She almost smiled. "Four in, four out."

The crawl pinched, turned mean, and opened just enough to choose between light and less light. She chose the less and felt the temperature drop. Water slicked the walls. The passage narrowed until the pack on his back rasped stone. He shrugged it off without breaking stride and shoved it forward to her reach. She dragged it while he took the drag on her belt with two fingers and kept her center while she worked the weight.

"Two more," Mireya said. She meant turns. She meant chances.

Something clicked over their heads. A thin red line walked a beam and paused as if sniffing. Zane lifted his hand above Elia's shoulder, not touching, close. The line brightened. He pulled back one finger width. It dimmed.

"Tuned to heat delta." She exhaled slow.

"Then stop breathing like you are on fire."

"Hard ask," he said, and she felt his smile without seeing it.

They reached the bend that would decide them. Pressure built teeth. She listened, not for sound, for the absence that comes before it. The gate's weight moved in the stone.

"Mark," she said, and shoved into the throat, shoulder first, making space for the people she refused to lose.

The gate hit where her head had been a breath ago, a flat clang that erased language.

SUBLEVEL
8

The last gate's clang still lived in Elia's bones when the tunnel shouldered them toward air. The vibration hummed along her teeth and scraped breath thin. They moved the way people learn in places that have no light. Mireya led because this route knew her and moved a little easier when she passed. Elia kept tight to her shoulder. Zane covered the rear with the kind of calm that meant he had already counted how many things could go wrong and had chosen the one he could break with his body if he had to. They did not speak. They counted breath, answered with taps, and let only the small animal sounds of living slip out into the dark.

At the final bend, Mireya pressed her palm to the hatch seam as if checking a fever, then turned. Her voice barely stirred the air.

"We split. Elia goes up. Her cover is primed. We need eyes above and a hand on what the upper grid hides behind glass. Zane comes with me. We cut a false trail through Ravine West and burn caches if we have to. The window is measured in hands and blood."

"I stay on the board," Kade said. "Windows only. If I go quiet, count thirty and turn west."

"Do you have both?" Mireya asked.

Elia nodded.

Zane lifted her wrist and tapped twice where the skin thinned over the pulse. She answered with two taps. It meant the same thing in both directions: *I hear you.*

Mireya climbed first. The hatch loosed a breath of rain and stone and diesel.

Elisabeth Nerr, according to the paper tucked in Elia's pocket, pulled up her hood and drew a clean lungful.

Zane tightened the strap of her mask with the same careful pressure he had used on a live wire 3 minutes earlier, the kind that would have betrayed them if it so much as hummed. It was not tenderness, not exactly; it was a promise written with steady hands that said he was not finished protecting what he had just asked for.

"Listen for my voice," she said.

He flinched at the word, as if a room had gone cold. "I will."

◄◄ ► ❚❚ ■ ►►

The Skyline Line wore the rain like jewelry. Chrome held the city's light and handed it back with a smoothness that felt like sanctioned thought.

Citrus solvent mixed with wet fabric inside the car. Ads glided along the glass with the same smile on different mouths.

A toddler gnawed a strap until a parent turned her gently without looking away from the comfort loop above the doors.

A man near the end blinked in time with the platform beacons, as if a small metronome had been set behind each eye.

Elia set her palm on a strap whose raised dots had been rubbed flat by a thousand thumbs. Her cuff blinked green with the man to her left and the woman to her right. She matched their breathing.

The forged ID laced under her skin fed the scanner on the beat, and the dead Band's shell returned the health pings it was built to mimic. Her heart refused the tempo and ran hot by a half count.

A drone's shadow passed along the window and vanished. The car shifted pressure without admitting to movement.

"Now arriving, Sanctum Gate," the overhead said in that soothing measure the city taught to infants.

Her fingers tightened. The name struck the soft parts of her and left a bruise. The city had retired that word in public. Hearing it here felt indecent. The carriage sighed to a stop, and even the sound of people stepping out breathed like rehearsal.

Above the rails, a glass room watched the city try to remember and worked harder to make it forget.

Aric stood with his hands behind his back so his spine could be a weapon even while he stood still. Screens fed him numbers and shapes and faces already converted into facts.

"This is not a glitch," Veren said. "It is a breach."

Aric did not answer; he had no habit of naming weather when he could use it.

"Reauthorize Sanctum," he said, and the command slid into the lattice and woke routines that should have stayed asleep.

At the back rail, Carrow stared at a feed without changing his face.

A profile ticked across a corner. Nerr, Elisabeth. The alias was correct. The woman was not. Green certification beads slid down the line like neat rain. "Ward," he said under his breath, speaking to bone more than air. "Inez warned me." He looked away before he could watch himself make the same mistake twice.

"Deploy beta agents," Aric said. "Seal egress."

The Protocol Architect did not look up as she altered parameters.

"Increase pair sensitivity. Tighten predictive sweeps when two signatures couple. Penalize proximity."

Aric flicked two fingers. "Do it."

Sanctum Gate turned its crowd into a river of even faces. Elia's cuff passed the arch with polite confidence. A drone hung above like a quiet god; she did not look up because the rules said she should not. The market that had replaced protests sold fruit that smelled like nothing and tasted like permission. Condensation ticked from a cracked canopy into bowls that had never known dirt. She let the current carry her to a heap of gray orbs. The woman behind the stall kept her eyes on her hands. Knuckles rose like knots under damp skin. A clear poncho clung to her shoulders and wore an old tape patch the color of nicotine.

"Delta's ash turned black," Elia said. She kept her voice soft and shaped it slightly wrong.

"Only if the fire breathes again," the woman replied. If you were not listening for the second river under the first, you would think it was about weather. A crease beside her mouth held the ghost of laughter that had been evicted years ago.

A coin touched the scale. A paper parcel slid across the worn wood. The weight in Elia's palm was wrong for fruit. The paper felt rough, not slick.

She stepped into the thin seam where a pillar met a wall and opened the wrap with a thumb. Old air breathed out. A key lay on her palm with honest teeth. Its shoulder carried two words the city had tried and failed to erase. Sublevel 8. Cold woke under her skin and spread like clear water. She slid the key into the inner seam of her coat and fastened the useless button that hid it.

Twice a scanner kissed her wrist and tried to read the history in her blood. Twice it found the story forgery had written ahead of time. She left the main corridor a heartbeat too early because breath belonged to her and not to them.

The service stair forgot to groan and felt newer than it was. She took the flights down and counted pipes by hand. On the landing where numbers peeled in scabs, she found a lock that had not been turned since the first uprising. The key moved as if guided by its own memory. The click ran up her bones and settled under her tongue.

Sublevel 8 had been peeled out of public language because names make pretending harder. The air tasted like old filters and tired plastic. Dust lay in an even sheet without the sweetness of decay. Towers of metal still blinked their tiny lights with the stubborn patience of machines that believed duty would one day be noticed. Most screens slept. One did not.

AXIOM NODE

Glowed in a corner. A hairline scratch on the casing had been polished by long habit, a small ritual of care someone had kept when care had fallen out of fashion.

School tried to surface. A teacher whose face would not hold still. Long words that felt like a mouthful of questions. Then the day Pulse pedagogy replaced all of it. Elia laid her palm on the glass. It was cool and did not push her away. The screen rolled out of its dream.

Text cut itself into the air. Not orders. Sentences with weight.

What if the Pulse keeps peace by holding it hostage?

What if Harmony was the first lie?

What if the ones who remembered how to feel were the first to go?

The skin along her arms lifted. She touched the list and it unfolded into faces. Not portraits. People trying to say something true before the system taught their mouths shame. She dragged a finger along the timeline and watched a chest fill with breath that had not been designed in a lab.

Along the bottom edge, a ribbon of system text jittered the way a nervous habit does. It read:

CRC FAIL

INDEX REBUILD

ARCHIVE MODE OFFLINE-LOCAL

In the margin, a diagnostic trembled and climbed like a fish testing the surface.

SPEAKER SIMILARITY

Rose and fell through:

0.62, 0.78, 0.71

Baseline sample incomplete

Flickered beside it. Another label tried to appear and then hid behind a red block.

HERITAGE MATCH

MATERNAL LINE

Refused to render. A small ear icon, crossed with a lock, blinked once and went still. She swallowed and kept her hand where it was.

A nameless file wore a lock like a smile that wanted to be believed. Elia slid the hash Mireya had taught her into the waiting field. The lock sighed and let go. A bar tried to be brave.

Decrypt 14%; 67%; Complete

The image that replaced the list was bad on purpose. Blacks were crushed to hide what mattered.

A man stood before the camera. He was younger than the name the city had given him, yet older than the trust he would need. His eyes held the sharp light that hurt finds right before it learns purpose.

"If you are watching this," he said, the microphone clicking where a finger had tapped it, "they failed to kill me entirely."

He did not blink for too long.

"They moved the voice out of the throat and into the wall. They took the name and called it an asset. They did not erase the memory of her."

Static crept along the line. "They modeled obedience on her cadence," he said.

The word fell into Elia like a key dropped down a well.

"It calms, it contains, it reuses what the body already trusts."

The diagnostic flashed an unhelpful number and then hid behind red blocks. A secondary meter woke like a guilty thought and then aborted.

"Copy it back into disobedience. Sanctum is not a vault. It is a weapon. They are building a core out of what remains of me."

The image iced and freed itself. His mouth shaped the beginning of a name that Elia's body recognized before her mind could name it.

"Her name is I—" Static tore the syllable. One clean line made it through.

"Find the pod. Break the feedback. Use her voice."

The room remembered it had other duties. A tone traveled inside the wall, the kind of sound buildings make when they recall their job.

◄◄ ► ❚❚ ■ ►►

Above her, Sanctum's core made a noise a human ear feels more than hears. A technician wiped sweat from her forehead with the inside of her wrist.

"It is aligning with the original lattice," she said, and the accuracy of the statement did not calm her.

"Initiate reintegration," Aric answered.

No one bothered with *sir*. Reinforced glass sheltered a pod that pulsed with pale light. Something inside twitched against the gel.

"Sedate it," Aric said. A readout changed color to prove compliance.

"It is mutating," someone tried.

"Keep it quiet," Aric said, quieter than before, the way people lower their voices to convince a machine the world is calm.

The Protocol Architect nudged the affect channels and watched the richness shrink.

"Pair spikes track to proximity events. Push recall prompts when heart rates couple."

Carrow studied the quiet on the sector map. Old tunnels pressed up against new concrete.

A maintenance shaft lived only in pencil because the clerk who should have transferred it into a program had died or left or been reassigned. He traced where Sublevel 8 ran beneath the archives and did not need to be told a seller had given a key to a girl with a name the system loved too much.

"Ward," he said to the glass. "Your mother told me we would arrive here." The glass did not argue or agree.

◄◄ ► ❚❚ ■ ►►

Old recall channels, the ones the grid claimed to have buried, lit up with a sound like a bruise being pressed. Mireya's shoulders lifted as if someone had poured ice down the back of her shirt.

Zane was already moving. He tore the cover off a tired set that wanted to be left alone and fed it a line. The screen woke and showed a symbol the modern net said was folklore. The first cells' mark rode a carrier wave no one should have been able to see.

"Someone woke an AXIOM node," he said.

"Elia," Mireya answered. She did not make it a question.

"They will trace it."

"Only if they can read dead languages," he said.
"You seem fluent." There was no time to spend on that.
"Get ready to pull her out."

◄◄ ► ❚❚ ■ ►►

Elia's cuff shifted from green to a warning amber and then admitted the truth and turned red. A small scarlet dot near the latch began to glow the way a siege tower used to. Drones spun up above her like midges finding a river at dusk. She closed the file and blacked the glass. The part of her that enjoyed outsmarting things stepped to the side. Speed took its place.

The corridor back to the service stair had not changed in 8 minutes. It would not show kindness now. She kept her pace fast without breaking into a run, because running makes a sound cameras like to study. She pushed the mask up until it bit the bridge of her nose and dropped her breathing low. Her eyes stayed on the seam where the wall met the floor, the narrow place where dust gathers and feels loyal.

A drone descended the service shaft with the restraint of a wasp that had been taught manners. Its beam traced the upper third of the wall. She flattened and slid through the dead air at the baseboard where dust had settled in a soft ridge. Her shoulders scraped and the scrape hurt and the hurt held her in the present.

On the second landing, a door that had never been asked to work so hard tried to move on orders traveling fast through wire. Elia set the key in a different lock with the arrogance of someone who had just watched a man explain the truth with his damaged voice. The key turned. The door exhaled and let her pass. She entered a maintenance duct built by someone with small shoulders and very little respect for comfort.

"Mask," she told herself, the word a switch for breath. "Low." She went to elbows and knuckles and moved forward.

A cable brushed her cheek and snapped static into her ear. The jolt cut her breath. Hypoxia narrowed the world, and the narrowing let something older through.

Hands cupped her jaw in a room that smelled of paper and rain. *Count my breaths,* a man had said, warm against her mouth, and she had answered with fours, the same measure she used now. The kiss-memory did not belong to this week. It belonged to a life that had been sanded down. She tried to see his jaw and found only light and the feeling of being recognized. The vision broke, yet its shape remained. She moved again.

Three slow breaths. Then move. Hands to the rail. Then drop. She slid through a vent and found the lip of a trench with her heel. Her calf clenched. She swallowed the sound, swung her weight, cleared by less than a breath, and kept going.

◄◄ ► ‖ ■ ►►

In the glass room, a technician said, "We have her," and the pronoun took on more work than it should.

"Bring her alive," Aric replied. Living assets outlast dead ones.

Carrow had already sent for the only unit who knew how to take a person without unspeaking her in the process. He knew where she would surface if she wanted air. He knew because 20 years earlier he had watched a different woman go into that same place and had learned exactly how the city encourages repetition.

Theta did not sleep. The gel cooled when a machine asked it to, yet rebuilt nerves did not know obedience. Eyelids lifted. The iris showed the map a harried tech had copied wrong. A sound moved into the vents that made a man swear and then pretend he had not. It was not a scream; a scream would have been kinder. It was a name pulled apart and threaded together again, like a child opening a toy to see how it works. "Elia," the sound said. The gel did not smother it.

"Seal it," Aric said. The pod hushed itself like a thing punished for a question.

◄◄ ► ▐▐ ■ ►►

Elia found the last hatch by pattern. Screws sat in a familiar square. A plate held fast, then gave. The dogs turned with a stubbornness she recognized. Rain breathed on the far side. Oil lifted to her tongue. She twisted and leaned and the hatch let go a little, then a lot, the way a person finally exhales. Night air grabbed her hair and threw it across her face. She rolled onto the grating. The sting in her bones felt honest. Kinetic lights along the parapet woke and looked at her. A drone sliced red across the rain. She pressed herself against a vent stack and told fear to set up somewhere else for the next 10 minutes because she had work.

Her sleeve vibrated with an old-pattern ping the grid pretended no one used. She cupped a hand to the unit.

"Marking grid," Zane said. The encryption thinned his voice, yet it was still his. "Two blocks north and one west. Drop to the bleeder shaft and wait for the count. Mask window is 90 seconds. Every call we make cuts 10. Mireya says you have 30 before the sector locks cascade."

He did not say her name. He did not have to.

"I read you," she breathed.

The roofline stepped down toward a service spine. Predictive sweeps brightened ahead of her in a slow pulse. The lattice had begun to learn.

Elia pried a heat-sink tile off a vent, warmed it with her palm, and slid it into a puddle. She perched her jacket's cuff on top to lend it a second signature. The scout beam slowed to consider the fake. She was already moving, knees soaked, mouth quiet against her mask.

"Mask credit 90," Kade reported. "Sweep adds two corners. Hold your count."

"Mask at 80," Zane said.

She crossed a skylight frame and fell to a lower parapet. Metal rang against her shoulder. She counted four in and four out and kept the ringing from owning her.

A drone nosed toward her heat where the metal broke the wind. She flattened along stone until the beam slid on. The Band shell warmed on her wrist as if it wanted to be part of her again. She ignored the traitor heat and threaded her path through the cold sheets where rain pooled.

"Mask at 70," Zane said. "A sweep passes east to west in 5. If the red coin touches you, hold breath."

"That is a hard ask," she whispered, and felt the shape of his smile even without seeing it.

The beam walked the parapet like a lazy vein. Elia flattened and dragged herself through the dead space under it by the strap of her pack. Steel hissed 2 roofs over and bit nothing. A second drone drifted high and dipped when her heat and the decoy crossed. She crouched beside a vent, warmed the plume with her hand, then stepped away. The drone chose the plume and dropped. Good. Learning could be taught the wrong lesson.

"Mask at 60," Zane said. "We pay for each whisper. Are you clear?"

"I am clear," she said.

She could vanish into the route they had planned, find Mireya and Zane, write a plan and rewrite it until someone was lost in a hallway that almost matched this one, and then live with it. Or she could accept the choice she had already made when the AXIOM clip told her the truth.

Sanctum was a weapon. The core was not only a machine. Her voice could crack it.

Across the rain, a building the city called maintenance blinked once in a way you see only when you train yourself to watch the wrong things. A service ladder fell into dark. A drone swung by and let its beam crawl the parapet like a snake remembering how to move.

Above her, the lattice adjusted again. Sweeps closed faster when two signatures coupled and slid when she broke contact with metal. She kept 1 boot on stone and the other on a rubber seam to muddy her trace.

She keyed the comm low. "Mark the grid," she whispered. "We are taking Sanctum apart."

"Mask at 50," Zane said. "Make it count."

"Count me."

"Four in, four out."

Elia set both hands on the ladder and started down into the throat of the city she meant to make honest. Rain turned to the smell of warm duct. The rungs were slick where a thousand uncounted hands had gone this way without being written down. Above, scout beams brightened and dimmed as if they were arguing with themselves. That, too, could be taught.

She let the word into the metal and the wire, not as a single note but as a direction.

"Override," she told the old lines that had carried a lie for too long. Then she went down, one careful rung at a time, toward the place where her voice would have work to do.

CONTAINMENT TWO

The trolley dropped like a thrown tool, wheels shrieking until steel found steel and turned fall into motion. The gust shoved air into their faces and left grit on their teeth. Mireya lay flat to sight the line by feel alone, her forearm braced against the wooden lip, her eyes moving the way they do when a map is inside bone. Zane rode the brake with one foot and the frame with the rest of him, weight set to take the next lie the tunnel might tell. Elia hooked an arm through a rung and let the shudder climb into her shoulders so the rest of her could be quiet.

"Curve in three," Mireya said, not loud, the voice of a person steadying a table before it spills. "We take the right-hand rail. The left is a bluff."

The trolley pitched, the right-hand rail answered, the world decided not to throw them. Ahead, the concrete went from echo to damp and back again, telling them where the space narrowed and where it would cough.

A slate taped to the trolley's lip blinked its unfriendly green. The city spoke through it in the language it prefers for comfort.

PREDICTIVE SWEEP: +2 CORNERS
PAIR SPIKE: LOW
MASK CREDIT: 90 s ON BREACH
VARIANCE PENALTY: NOMINAL

"Variance stable," Kade said into the shudder. "I'll bounce one trace into the dead conduit when you call 'trace.'"

They coasted into a cut-out that had once been a service bay. Pipes sweated overhead. A sign scabbed by time still pretended to be useful. Mireya held the trolley with one hand and the chamber with the other.

"Three objectives," she said, the kind a room can hold even when it shakes. "Decoy, breach, extraction. Zane and I run the heat off your path. Elia, you thread the spine. The dampener buys you ninety seconds of being no one. Each call costs ten. We keep the rest off you."

Elia checked the small pack again, thumb to clasp, the motion automatic the way a person rechecks the front door even when they know they turned the lock. Zane held out the dampener cable. Their hands met. Brief, practical, unarguable—a pulse mapped to a task.

"If the window narrows faster than we thought, you don't stay to teach the system about mercy," he said.

"I'll get out.," she said. He nodded once, the only answer that didn't waste air.

Mireya's mouth lifted in something almost like approval and then interest snapped the expression shut.

"Count," she said, and the board lit on the breath of the word.

A thread-thin loop crackled in Elia's ear, the one Joren had preloaded before they left safe air. He had pulled the chord out of the speeches and built a spine from the way sentences sit when the Architect speaks. The clip didn't say words yet.

Elia stood in the narrow and let the sound meet her. She set tongue to palate where remembered cadence waits and opened the vowel the way the Architect had trained a city to hear it. The first pass landed close and finished wrong. Her ending softened when it should have been clean. The slate shook its head in numbers.

SPEAKER SIMILARITY: 0.81 → 0.74
VARIANCE PENALTY: RISING

"Again," she said, and this time took the breath at four, not three. She added the small nothing between the second and third beat, the space you hear when a person is about to say a dangerous word and decides to offer it gently.

Zane didn't correct her voice. He didn't take sound from mouth. He stood close enough that she could count the lift and fall in his chest.

"Four in," he said, quiet enough only the space between them could hear. "Hold the last half-beat before you drop. Don't let the end carry your truth."

"How would you know that?" she asked. The question carried more weight than the lesson could justify.

He answered with something almost like a smile and not at all like a joke. "Because you taught me to breathe when rooms forgot how."

Mireya's hand came up, two fingers—the count they'd agreed would interrupt anything short of blood loss. "Sweep is moving," she said. "Predictive just learned our corners."

PREDICTIVE SWEEP: +3 CORNERS

MASK CREDIT: −10s

Elia took the breath Zane had given back to her and set it between her teeth so she wouldn't drop it.

"Ready," she said. "Needle."

The corridor beyond the bay had the meanness of a space meant for machines. The lights didn't pretend to be for humans. The skin on her forearms lifted at the change in air when the lattice raised its hackles.

PAIR SPIKE: MODERATE

Zane let one pace of distance open between them; the measurement readjusted.

PAIR SPIKE: LOW

She wanted him closer and didn't ask for it. The system was learning where proximity hurt it most.

The spine they needed had once fed maintenance carts and law. The door that guarded it had learned, like many doors in this city, to be proud of doing what it was told. Elia set the dampener at the seam and felt it kiss the signal from her. Mask credit began to bleed. The clock didn't tick; it breathed.

MASK CREDIT: 90, 80, 70

"On my voice," she said—not a command, an agreement to meet in a place she could hold.

She shaped the opening phrase the way the Architect had trained the wall to accept it—not meaning, angle. The port listened, argued, then softened the exact amount a person softens when a trusted cadence walks in and says everything is under control. Her stomach turned at the taste of that trust. The panel smiled green in the idiotic way of machinery doing a job well. The door breathed open.

Beyond it, the air tasted of clean technology and old harm. The core chamber sat like a heart in a chest told to beat to a foreign rhythm. Glass where there should have been kindness. Light where there should have been quiet. The pod held a human shape in gel and tubes the city refused to name. Readouts ran in columns, terrible because they were accurate.

REINTEGRATION
FEEDBACK
FUSION

Under them the numbers jittered where numbers rarely do.

The sound the building made when it saw her wasn't a siren. It was a small discipline, the tone you use to tell a child to sit up straight.

CONTAINMENT TWO: ENGAGE
PREDICTIVE SWEEP: +4 CORNERS
MASK CREDIT: 60

Theta's eyes opened the way a stage light warms— slow, then certain. He saw her, and something in his face collected itself from scattered places. For a moment no machine mattered because the body recognized presence as the first truth it ever learned. His palm lifted. Glass met skin. She set her own hand to his. The cold asked a question. Heat answered.

"I have you," she said. The monitors tried to translate that into something useful and failed.

Zane moved to the console and let his fingers fail to find the keyboard that wanted him. He didn't touch the commands; he didn't trust a language that would rewrite what a body intended to do.

"Mask credit at forty," he said. "If you're going to teach it doubt, do it now."

Elia's throat felt like stone and rain. She lifted her chin and spoke the prompt in the same cadence she had practiced with the van's ceiling inches above her head. She didn't argue with Sanctum. She walked through it. The first line settled the surface. The second slid under the skin. The third found the place where the algorithm had built its nest. "Harmony is the name you gave to obedience," she said, and the sound did what she asked of it, not what the wall had been told to do to her.

SPEAKER SIMILARITY: 0.89 → 0.93
VARIANCE PENALTY: HIGH
FEEDBACK ERROR: ASCENDING

The room updated its own fear.

CONTAINMENT TWO: LOCKDOWN

The door behind them thought about closing. Zane put a shoulder into it and didn't let it learn new habits.

Theta's breath shortened. He closed his eyes like a man listening for a forgotten step on old stairs. "They told me I was an instrument," he said, naming a smaller sin to reach the larger one. "They taught my mouth to count the city's sleeping." His hand on the glass curled, a fraction only. "You made the counting mean something again."

Something low and reckless in her answered. Zane's voice arrived with his own risk folded inside it. "You can carry the end if you take it back from where they learned it," he said to Elia. "You gave me the words in a room with paper and rain, when I thought I'd lost the last useful thing I was. You stood at a window, and I told you I wasn't afraid to love you, and you told me to count until the fear left the room. Four in, four out. You said vows like they were a tool. I've known your cadence longer than my own name."

The wall tried to eat the words and make them a dataset.

SPEAKER SIMILARITY: 0.96
HERIT—MATCH: MATER—LINE REDACTED
VARIANCE PENALTY: CRITICAL

Elia's vision brightened at the edges. She kept speaking. She made the last turn of the key and didn't let the truth in her tone ride the ending. The algorithm had learned the Architect's mercy; she gave it an older version of care—the kind that doesn't soothe, the kind that expects a self to stand.

The pod shuddered. Not a malfunction. A refusal. Readouts that had layered obedience over memory broke their own lines.

FEEDBACK LOOP: FRACTURED
REINTEGRATION: FAILED

Theta's mouth formed a word and this time the city didn't sand the edges off the sound. "Elia," he said. His eyes cleared in the way eyes do when pain becomes honest. The seal on the hatch released. The gel sighed like a laboratory shamed into telling the truth.

MASK CREDIT: 20

Numbers didn't care about their moment. Zane caught the hatch with both hands and turned his back to it so it wouldn't close on her shoulders. Mireya's voice came on a ribbon of air so thin it shouldn't have held. "North hall closing in two. Predictive is inside our plan."

Elia slid gloved fingers under the tube at Theta's throat and cut it where cut would do least harm. He flinched and then controlled the flinch. She set an arm under his and his weight told her more than any file. Built for compliance, rebuilt for endurance, still a man who could choose. They moved—exact, not fast.

Zane stepped into the first path a drone would expect and offered it heat and motion. Elia kept Theta near the wall where sensors miss.

The corridor that had welcomed them turned stubborn. Locks hissed like cats.

PAIR SPIKE: HIGH

PREDICTIVE SWEEP: +5 CORNERS

CONTAINMENT TWO: ACTIVE

Zane handed the dampener to Theta without looking away from the next angle. "Against your pulse," he said. "Two breaths. No more. We need the rest."

Theta obeyed as if the command had come from memory. The slate counted down without grace.

MASK CREDIT: 10, 9, 8

"Red coin ahead," Kade warned. "Take the cold seam under the pipe."

They hit the choke tunnel, built narrow for utility and kept narrow by habit. The air thinned with static the way a page goes thin with age. Elia swallowed and felt her body decide to do something without being asked. The first slide of hypoxia turned the world to copper and light. Behind it a room stood up—the smell of paper warmed by a radiator and rain beaten out of a coat hung on a hook.

A man's hands guided her shoulders, not possession, a check. "Count my breaths," he said, and it was Zane's mouth without the scar, his eyes without the night they had been forced to carry. Four in, four out. Vows without ceremony. Her mouth answered because the body remembers what matters and refuses to release it, no matter how cleverly a city writes over it.

She returned to the present with a breath she could use. The drone at the end of the choke found the first corner of her heat, then lost it to a vent Zane had warmed two steps ago.

"Left," she said, and they didn't argue. Mireya's shot was a whisper in the heavy air. A machine dropped where it hovered and decided to die without making a fuss.

The lift shaft they'd used to come down had changed loyalties. A gate slid across the mouth, pleased with itself. Zane jammed a wrench where a proper tool should have gone and made the metal relearn humility. He held it because the gate hated being taught and would try to forget the lesson.

"Go," he said, without the shove a different man might have put on the word. Elia and Theta took the space his body bought.

The trolley line wasn't the one they had left. Sanctum had learned to reshape the inside of itself. A new red line crawled the wall where diagrams used to sit.

CONTAINMENT TWO: COLLAR
PREDICTIVE SWEEP: +6 CORNERS

The city was closing its fingers.

Mireya ran two hallways ahead to break the habit of the map. She placed heat where it would be mistaken for more of them and shut down a row of lights in a way that made the grid waste a scan on emptiness.

"Mask credit at zero," she said, because telling the truth keeps people alive. "We are ourselves again."

The trolley waited where they'd left it because it didn't know how to betray. Elia put her back into the lever and felt

Theta's hands join her, steady and strong. Zane arrived with his breath sawed short and a cut on his cheek that would dry into a line by morning. The trolley jumped forward into speed like a body remembering how to run. The alarm behind them tried to turn itself into a wall. It couldn't keep up.

The tunnel did what tunnels do when four bodies—one newly returned to his name—threw weight and intention down the line. It became a wind instrument. The air made a sound like a long held note. Elia watched the slate as if it were a pulse.

PREDICTIVE SWEEP: +3 CORNERS
PAIR SPIKE: MODERATE
VARIANCE PENALTY: STABLE

She looked at Zane because the numbers had nothing useful to say about what she needed. He looked back and gave the small nod that says keep breathing; I'll take the next harm if it comes from that angle.

They cleared the last bend the model had drawn and entered space the computer hadn't learned yet. The trolley rumbled over a joint that hadn't been kind in years. The sound went up the tunnel like thunder and came back as a rumor. Mireya's laugh broke out low, the sound a person makes when the world offers a little proof that work pays.

◄◄ ► ❚❚ ■ ►►

Aric stood in his glass cage and watched a shape on the central screen that didn't look like a map. The ring of containment tightened and loosened as if something inside had learned to breathe. He didn't say *stabilize*; he no longer believed the system responded to tone.

"Close the west apron," he said. His voice had the weight of a tool hitting a bench.

The technician didn't ask a question. Carrow stood one pace back and told a door to stay open that the system had asked to shut—not because he had chosen sides in any noble sense, but because he could live with that choice. He didn't call it mercy. He didn't call it anything.

◄◄ ► ❚❚ ■ ►►

The trolley shuddered into the old spur where a hand pump still hung like an apology from a different century. Zane was off first. He took the handle and yanked. The switch answered with a sound that pleased nobody, the rail clicked over, and the metal gave them a route the model hadn't predicted. They rode it a dozen meters, braked hard, and bailed to a rusted side door that let onto a service passage.

They cut through a shop that had died without witnesses—counters bare, pegboard marked with the absence of tools. The air there tasted like copper pennies and patience. Mireya paused at the threshold long enough to hear if a trap wanted to introduce itself. The silence offered nothing useful. She pointed with her chin. Zane went, shoulders angled to catch attention that would otherwise land on Elia's spine. Theta took the middle, one hand on the wall to hide the tremor.

A drone's red beam searched the mouth of the alley they needed to cross. The vent they'd warmed earlier still pushed heat like a tired animal. The beam slid off the wrong truth and went looking for the right one somewhere else. Elia felt her skin sit fully on her bones again. Not safety—ownership.

"West," she said. The word moved them. The city dropped a gate as if it had been waiting for that syllable. The plate fell and met pavement where her head would have been if the time had been a fraction different. The crash sent grit into their mouths and stole language for a breath. They kept going because stopping is a habit the city loves and they didn't intend to be loved.

Ahead, a rusted plate brooded in a wall that had been painted six institutional colors. Elia set her fingers into the seam where someone with a secret had expected a hand like hers. The plate shifted with a sound like coins. A narrow stair showed itself, stone worn to a dip in the middle. They dropped single file—elbows, heels, webbing, breath. At the bottom a hand-pumped trolley slept on rails the color of old blood.

"Now," Mireya said.

Zane swore a smile and put shoulder and spine to the lever. Theta joined without instruction. The lock screamed itself open like a thing taught to be difficult. The rail answered the argument with movement. Above them a door slammed and hesitation left a group of men who had been paid to remove hesitation from their bodies.

Elia threw the brake, Zane yanked the chain, Theta drove the lever forward. The trolley surged into the dark. A shot found concrete and died doing what it thought was work. A red wash hit vapor in an old purge line and bloomed into its own blind. The tunnel swallowed the wash and took the rest of the noise. The slate blinked once more before the signal died, as if the city couldn't help being honest when it was losing track.

PREDICTIVE SWEEP: LOST

CONTAINMENT TWO: HOLD

They didn't cheer. They counted the next bend. They counted the one after. Mireya's voice came even, not tired, exactly right for the moment.

"Point 12 in sixty," she said. "We keep moving until the street agrees we exist."

Theta set his hand over the dampener where it had bruised a weak vein the city found convenient. He looked at Elia with the bewildered wonder of a man who has been returned something simple and not at all small. "They built a machine that could use my breath," he said. "You gave it back to me."

Zane angled his body so she could take the sentence without being seen doing it. She closed her hand on the rail and felt grit print into her palm. "We finish it," she said to both of them, and the words sat down on the trolley like weight worth carrying.

Rain started somewhere ahead, the honest kind. The tunnel narrowed to a throat and opened into a service mouth lined with wet brick. Mireya lifted two fingers and counted them through the last bend. The trolley jolted onto the spur at Point 12, brakes screaming, and coasted under a hinged grate someone had forgotten to lock. Zane was out first and hauled the grate with both hands while Elia and Theta slid past into the alley's wet light. The grid hummed above them like a hive remembering its sting.

"West apron in thirty," Mireya said, already moving.

Zane brushed Elia's wrist where the dampener had bit and found her pulse steady. "Count me," he said.

"Four in, four out," she answered, and the words put their feet on the ground for them.

They cleared the mouth of the alley as a red wash rolled over the roofline and the city tried to close its hand. No one looked back. They took the open street and disappeared into the rain.

CHAPTER 18
COUNT OF FOUR

Rain stitched the street into one sheet and kept stitching after they were gone. They cut the service gap Mireya liked, took the last bend low, and pushed through the bunker door with steam lifting off jackets. Wet metal bit the nose. Heat pooled around the conduit cabinet. Water ran off the map table in thin lines.

Theta stood near center with his arms loose and shoulders set, useful-straight, not parade-straight. The borrowed shirt stretched across a frame trained by a building, not a house. Faces ringed him at careful angles that turned fear into prudence. Zane wore a short pacing curve into the floor beside the cabinet, heel pivoting on the same scuff he always found when nerves needed work. Mireya leaned spine to steel, arms folded, mouth idle until words earned it. Elia slid off the carrier pack, set the dampener on the table with a steady hand, and took the space between them without a speech.

"Say it plain," someone near the wall said.

"Weapon or fuse?"

"Fuse until we make it a bridge," Kade said, not leaving the lattice. "I've got Point 12 idle if you need ground."

Theta met the room. "They trained a loop to eat names and reuse what broke," he said. "You cracked it long enough to step me out. That crack sits where the loop feeds. We can touch it again."

Mireya kept it clean. "You hunted us."

"They used me," he said. "I chose to remember."

Heat crawled under Zane's collar. He cut in before the room picked a target. "He's here. That counts more than a test none of us pass with this clock."

The console Zane had bullied into life coughed, flickered, then steadied into a thin ribbon of the city's thinking. His hand on the analog bridge kept it honest.

Theta hovered over keys without touching. He never trusted an interface that tried to make him relax. Text arranged itself with knife-calm.

CLEANSE/QUEUE: OUTER_DISTRICTS/UNVERIFIED →SCHEDULED
FILTER_PROFILE: ARCH_MERCY →ARCH_NEUTRAL
BEHAVIOR_FLAGS: DREAM_DIVERGENCE | CALIBRATION_FAIL | GUIDANCE_LATENCY
ACTION: ERASE/REASSIGN

"They won't send squads if they can teach a city to forget it asked for help," Theta said. "Cleanse rides the bands. Miss a calibration, the log flags you as unwell. Clinics become recovery pods. Subliminals tighten. Dream scripts cut off the wrong endings. Then the record calls that care."

Mireya tracked time. "When does the queue hit bodies."

Theta tipped his chin at the stamp march. "It started. Outer blocks fold now. Erasures file as treatment."

Elia leaned into the console heat until it sang in her forearms. "How many times can you touch their process before the hand gets tagged."

"Once clean," he said. "I can reclass a subsystem to audit and make it waste a minute proving it behaves. Do it twice and the system eats the tool and my access."

"Spend it," she said.

Theta's fingers moved. A subpanel hiccuped into audit. The queue stuttered at one nurse station for one long breath. A bus stop full of gray coats stayed upright instead of folding.

◀◀ ▶ ❚❚ ■ ▶▶

A tower full of cold liked the sound of heels that did not slam. Screens stacked like weather. Aric held his hands behind his back. His spine carried the voice he never raised. Advisors in white lined the rail in a clean row.

"Report," he said.

SANCTUM BREACH: ACKNOWLEDGED
ASSET THETA: MISSING
INFLUENCE WAVE: DETECTED
(ORIGIN: LEGACY LAYER)

"Accelerate," he said, and the syntax obeyed.

CLEANSE/QUEUE: OUTER_DISTRICTS/UNVERIFIED
→ ACTIVE
FILTER_PROFILE: ARCH_MERCY →ARCH_NEUTRAL
→ ARCH_SEVER

A door light in the lower feed held yellow longer than a tech liked, then flipped to:

PENDING INVESTIGATION

Carrow's thumb left the edge of his tablet. The blue vein on his hand went flat. He closed two routes the model loved, opened a dusty maintenance seam by calling it a calibration bypass, and filed it with a miser's words so no one would chase it. A team asked for confirmation.

"Proceed," he said, and let the word carry three sins and one debt.

⏪ ▶ ⏸ ⏹ ⏩

"Three objectives," Mireya said, tapping paper because the room had grown allergic to screens. "Decoy, breach, extraction. Kade, mast for a two-second sub-audible, clean carrier only. Make the model bite heat in the wrong place. Theta, bounces the trace once into a dead conduit to buy seconds. Elia, threads the under-stair to Core Tower and speaks from the throat. Zane and I take whatever the grid throws off that line. The mask window taxes words. Every syllable costs."

Theta nodded. "The bounce works once. They blacklist the conduit and me after that."

Zane passed Elia the dampener cable. Their fingers met, brief and solid. He checked a shoulder strap that didn't need checking. The strap wasn't the point. "If the window collapses faster than the math, you don't stay to teach them grace."

"I don't plan to die in a hallway," she said.

They turned for the door. Elia caught his sleeve. "Zane."

Tools went quiet. Joren stared at the floor. Mireya held the frame. Theta watched the feed.

She faced him. "Library weather. The chipped blue mug under the radiator. Four in, four out. The nick where your ring sat. Tell me I'm wrong."

His jaw set. "You walked into that room on purpose. I told you they would turn your voice into a tool. You said fast in, fast out, together. Bands took you from the chair and then from every file. I stood in that hall with your name on my tongue and kept it there so they didn't finish you."

"I signed it. I asked you to back me."

"I did," he said. "It still broke me. They pumped your cadence through lifts and trains. Kids slept under it and woke soft. Mothers pressed bands to glass and thanked the grid for your breath. I stood on a roof and kept my mouth shut. I wanted to rip the wires and I didn't."

She touched the pale ring scar. "You wore it for us."

"For the room with books and the heater that never quit," he said. "For the plan. I took it off the night you passed in a train window and I froze."

Her decoy band warmed under his hand. He held his ground. She didn't pull away.

He pressed his forehead to hers. Anger in his face. Care with it. "I loved you," he said. "I hated the choice you made me hold."

"I remember," she said. "I remember us. I know I loved you too." She took his collar in both hands and kissed him.

Heat off wet cloth. Salt and metal from the cut at his lip. His hand found her jaw. The other slid to the back of her neck. He steadied, then met her with the need she carried into the room.

She broke for air. He caught her strap and pulled her back. The second kiss landed harder. She fisted his jacket. He set his palm to her chest and felt the drum he had guarded by staying silent. He stopped with his mouth close. "I loved you first."

"I hear you."

He held her there. "You chose the dive. I carried the harm. I kept you alive by letting you think we had never met. I still hate the cost."

"I take it back," she said. "You don't pay it twice."

"Then hear me," he said. "Do not run at a wall to prove you can. Do not step into a beam to make a point. Come back when I count you home."

"Walk with me and keep me honest," she said. "You don't shrink me."

"I won't," he said. "I take the first hit if it buys you one breath that carries the line we need. Gate, beam, blade. Your voice breaks locks my body can't."

"Count me."

"Four in."

"Hold."

"Four out."

Mireya's shadow crossed the table. "We move."

◄◄ ► ❚❚ ■ ►►

Liran's mast rose out of alley water like a rib someone forgot to hide. The base sat in a rusted box meant to keep hands off and failed at it. Theta dropped to a knee at the legacy switcher and threaded the carrier into lines that had retired without honor. Zane watched the mouth of the alley in door-sized slices and marked who wasn't there. Mireya picked angles as if she hung them with string.

The model did its job.

PREDICTIVE_SWEEP: +2 CORNERS → +3 (Δ15 s)
PAIR_SPIKE: HIGH @ 1.5 m PROXIMITY
SPEAKER_SIMILARITY: 0.94 → 0.91

The first drone rushed and went blind on the flare Zane snapped off the brick with a throw his body knew by heart. The second moved lower and dragged its beam across the alley at a height that would have cooked Elia's hands. Zane shoved the spare accelerant under the mast and shot it as the pulse hit. Heat bloomed. The signature lied to a machine that loved heat more than sentences. Fire climbed the rig. Steam blew off the rain in sharp bursts. Mireya picked the old unit out of the sky with one clean shot. The third beam kissed through the bent door plate Zane had lifted, burned his shoulder deep, and left his breath rough for two counts before he set it right.

Elia lit the stove cup. Blue flame held steady. She cut fabric, cleaned the white edge out of the burn, wrapped the joint, and said, "Count to ten."

He hit seven with a curse he kept in his throat, hit ten with his jaw tight, and let her knot the strip. She touched her forehead to his for one beat. Steam slid under the moment and took it.

"Carrier up in three," Theta said, knuckles white on a knob he refused to fear. "Ladder on two. Cut heat left on one."

Elia set the sub-audible against her teeth and let it into the line like medicine the body finally accepts. For two seconds the word walked rooms where nothing personal had been allowed. It left prints the model could not scrub without admitting the surface.

REMEMBER.

Screens snapped back. Bands smoothed. A thousand hairline cracks stayed in place.

"Heat cut," Theta said, fingers wrapping the trace in a dead conduit like bad news in clean paper. The model lunged for the wrong corner and bit old metal.

They moved before correction. The maintenance seam Carrow had reclassed as a calibration bypass sat where a wall never forgave its door. Elia slid them through. The air refused perfume. Metal scraped truth along the teeth.

"Thirty breaths," Theta said, and this time it sounded like a receipt.

Elia counted. She took the stairs by twos. The decoy band warmed when Zane shouldered past to take the first angle.

The service bay at the foot of Core Tower pretended it did not belong to money. Oil and bleach fought for the nose. Theta set his palm to a panel that thought it was a wall and woke old recognition in the metal. The seam gave with a sound that respected itself. The under-stair curved down. The sound inside it had weight. Buildings with egos give even their vibrations rank.

The round throat room had no doors on purpose. Sound wanted one voice. Zane stepped into the first angle where a beam would land. Mireya took the second with a rifle that had outlived three owners.

"Carrier clean for two," Kade said. "On your close—keep the end neat."

Elia walked to center and set her breath as the first fact in the room. Theta tuned the carrier with a hand that hated how good it had become at making machines act human.

"On you," he said.

Elia didn't copy the Architect's mercy. She laid down an older kind of care that asked a self to stand. "If fear sits beside you, breathe with me—four in, hold, four out—until it leaves."

The wall tried to label tone.

SPEAKER_SIMILARITY: 0.91 → 0.93 → 0.88
TOLERANCE_PROFILE: KEY_SHIFT →
ARCH_NEUTRAL+
FEEDBACK_ERROR: ASCENDING

The model flattened its key. Theta pressed his palm harder to hold the carrier on line. A charge went at the turn and blew white noise into the room. Theta stepped into it with his shoulder like a man holding a door for a line of tired workers. Elia finished the sentence the city would spend years denying took place in this room.

On Aric's central screen the ring of containment stuttered, corrected, then drew a waveform that did not resemble any map his staff loved.

"Trace," Theta said. He said it again to move feet.

Zane bought the first step by standing where a cautious man would duck. Mireya bought the second with an angle that put a beam into concrete. They took the garbage stair because garbage always knows where it goes.

They came up in a room painted so often the layers curled like bark. The door had never learned to lock. It kept the habit. Zane set his hand on the wall to share weight; Elia took his wrist down and laid a fresh strip over the bandage with the same steady hands she had used under the mast. Outside, the grid hummed like a hive that remembered its sting.

Mireya's chin drew a route in the air. "We keep moving," she said. "Under their floor until the model draws the wrong corners and forgets to redraw them in time."

Elia met their eyes and let those looks stack into a place to stand. "Prime Core next," she said. "Masks on. Packs tight. Count of four. Thirty breaths."

Zane gave one small nod and made it mean more than any speech. "Four in," he said.

"Hold," she said.

"Four out."

The door took her shoulder. The corridor answered with motion. Rain waited above them and did not ask what they planned to break next.

CHAPTER 19
PRIME CORE

They moved before dawn. The uniforms didn't fit. A sleeve covered Zane's knuckles. Theta's collar pressed his throat. Mireya's patch showed the wrong decade. Elia kept her hood low. No band glowed on her wrist. The scanners tried to place her and returned silence.

Core Tower's lobby washed them through with workers who had learned to show nothing. Security doors opened on a steady rhythm. Theta palmed an old card at the service lift and let the light go green. They dropped two levels, then three. Air lost polish. Floors picked up grit. Sound shifted from public hum to machine work.

They cleared a utility corridor under the show floors. The walls carried data. Panels whispered. The building pushed a tone along the ducting that targeted breath and heart. Irritation ticked in Zane's jaw. Elia clocked it and touched his sleeve once. The decoy band under her cuff warmed at the contact. She let her hand fall and counted her breath on four to set the pace. Theta watched telemetry spill across a maintenance screen.

"Badge drift in your favor," Kade whispered. "Janitorial pass replicates at the turnstile in six."

"They're running affect cues," he said. "Short fear bursts. Mild disgust. It nudges choices. It cuts courage in the hall and increases compliance at a badge reader."

"Can you kill it here," Mireya asked.

"Only for this hall," he said. "It shifts nodes every ninety seconds."

"Then we do not stand still," Elia said.

The service stair dropped them to the under-stair throat. Sound carried here. It sat in ribs. A single ring of glass marked Prime Core access. Two guards sat inside the ring. Bored, upright. Theta slid a folder under the slot with an old work order and an inspection stamp from a retired division. The nearer guard scanned, checked Theta's collar, and made a choice that exposed obedience. He buzzed the door. They passed. He forgot their faces after they cleared the line.

Zane checked corners. He favored his burned shoulder. His jaw set when a step jarred it. Elia caught that step and changed her path to cut the jolt. The next turn held a low door with a broken latch and a storage sign nobody obeyed. She keyed it shut behind them. No cameras. A mop sink. Two shelves. A strip light stuttered, then burned steady.

"Jacket," she said.

He shrugged it off. Fabric had fused to skin at one corner. She boiled water on a pocket coil and soaked a strip. She slid the cloth under the edge and lifted in small pulls until the stuck part let go. He gripped the rack and breathed with her count. Four in. Hold. Four out. His breath settled. She cleaned the burn and set a new wrap from her sleeve. He watched her hands and let his shoulders loosen.

She stepped close. She set her palm on his jaw. He met her eyes and let the wall drop out of his face.

"Say stop," he said, their rule.

"I won't," she said. She touched his jaw. "My name isn't Ward."

His mouth tightened, then opened on the truth. "Elia Calder. You're my wife."

Air left her chest in a hard sweep. "Say it again."

"You're my wife."

She took his collar in both hands and pulled him in.

Their mouths found heat and stayed. He cupped her face and deepened the kiss until the work in his shoulders let go. She tugged his shirt up; it fell. Scars crossed his chest in short white lines. She traced each one and learned the map again. He watched and did not rush her.

She dropped her coat, then her shirt. Skin took the room from the metal. He looked at her; memory stood up in his face. She let him see. He stepped in. They kissed again and kept it. His thumb pressed the pulse at her throat. She set his hand flat and felt it answer.

He found the fastenings at her waistband. She hooked his belt and pulled. Cloth slid. Boots thumped the floor. He eased her back, then changed his mind and brought her down with him, exact, careful of the shoulder she had just wrapped. She climbed over him and took his mouth until thought fell away. He rolled, braced through the good arm, and drew her close. She set her knees, gripped his back, and met him with the same need that had carried her out of the dark.

"Tell me to stop," he said into her neck.

"Don't stop," she answered, and pulled him in.

Bodies set a rhythm they already knew. No performance. No distance. She held his gaze and kept it. He studied the lines of her face and did not look away. Her breath hitched, steadied, then rose. He counted under it because that had always been his job. Four in. Hold. Four out. He matched her until the count turned to sound and the sound turned to heat that filled the small room and shook the door on its hinges.

She gasped, tightened, then stilled under his hands. He followed her there and let the stillness take him. The kiss deepened and steadied until both of them could breathe again. He pressed his forehead to hers and held. She ran her fingers through his wet hair and learned the new salt at his temple.

She eased down. She wrapped him again. She pulled her shirt on and tied the knot with a firm tug. She tucked his collar and sealed the jacket across the dressing. He kissed the center of her palm. They listened at the door. Hall noise stayed flat.

Elia checked the color in his face and the set of his mouth. He lifted her pack, set the strap right, then kept his hand there a breath longer.

"Count me," he said, not for comfort, for contact.

"Four in," she said. "Hold. Four out."

He kissed her once more, brief and sure, and opened the door.

Mireya lifted two fingers and moved.

"We move," Mireya said in Elia's comm. "North stair two turns. Watch the second step. It rocks."

Elia looked once at Zane and set them back into the current.

The throat opened into the Prime Core antechamber. The room treated people as equipment. No décor. No windows. One main node. Three secondary racks. One console still wearing the AXIOM logo under a strip of black tape. Theta took the side terminal and tuned the carrier with his hand on metal. He kept his eyes off the nicer console; that one logged posture and blink rate.

"Two-second window for clean carrier," he said. "Then the lattice counters. I can bounce trace into a dead conduit on the west spine once. After that they blacklist it and my name with it."

Mireya nested by the cross-corridor with her rifle low. Zane took the angle at the door. The panel above the node fed the building's intent in clean lines.

PREDICTIVE_SWEEP: +2 → +3

PAIR_SPIKE: HIGH at 1.5 m

AFFECT_VECTOR: FEAR ↑

DOUBT ↑

The room pushed a tone that tried to place weight behind Elia's ribs. She set her stance and let breath roll through. Four in. Hold. Four out. The pressure lost purchase. She nodded to Theta.

"On you," she said.

He lifted two fingers and counted. On one, the carrier stood in the wire. On two, he locked it. On three, he pointed at her.

She stepped into the center. Her voice stayed steady and practical. No sermon. No lilt. A tool.

"If fear sits beside you, breathe with me. Four in. Hold. Four out. Hold again. Keep that count until your thoughts stop marching where you did not tell them to go. You are not broken. You are not alone."

The node tried to map her breath to the Architect's key. The readout drifted and fought.

SPEAKER_SIMILARITY: 0.92 → 0.89 → 0.93
TOLERANCE_PROFILE: KEY_SHIFT ↑
FEEDBACK_ERROR: RISING

The lattice narrowed the channel. Theta pinned the carrier with his palm and took a low shock. He set his jaw and kept his hand down.

"Hold the close," Zane said from the door. "Keep the end clean."

Elia finished the line without sweetness. She kept her truth out of the last beat. The panel showed stress where it shouldn't.

FEEDBACK_LOOP: FRACTURE
REINTEGRATION: FAIL FLAG

Core Tower pushed a heavier tone. Gloom tried to flood the antechamber. Zane's anger flashed, then broke on the count and fell away. Mireya's eyes watered for a beat; she blinked it clean and held her sights.

"Trace," Theta said. "They have us."

"Bounce it," Elia said.

He cut the heat left and wrapped the trace in the dead conduit. The model lunged for the wrong corner and lost them for a beat.

The wall slid. Two enforcers stepped through with visors low. Zane drew them to him without sound. He moved into their angle so their beams burned concrete. Mireya took the near visor and dropped him with a controlled pair. The second chose the wrong door and committed to it. Elia walked her line to the exit while Theta carried the carrier with his hand on the plate, jaw tight. They cleared the frame. The alarm found them again.

They ran the under-stair. The building adjusted. Red pins stacked along the spine.

FALLBACK_LATTICE: SPINUP

AFFECT_VECTOR: HASTE ↑ then REGRET ↑

Guilt hit hard. It said go back and fix the last thirty seconds. Elia felt it and moved through on the count. She set a hand to Zane's sleeve when his foot slowed. The band warmed. He shook off the drag and gave her a nod that landed as a promise.

They reached the blast hall. The door ahead had never failed a test. It failed open for three seconds. Theta stared at the panel.

"Gift's not mine," Kade said. "Take it anyway."

"Carrow," Theta said.

"No more gifts," Mireya said. "We move before the room changes its mind."

They moved. Core Tower corrected. Silver doors dropped from ceiling and floor. The last door hit the slot before the three cleared. Zane saw it coming and did the math. He stepped back on purpose, grabbed the manual lock with his good hand, and drove the pin through the housing. The door slammed, bent against the pin, and held. His body stayed on the wrong side.

Elia turned. She hit steel with both palms. He set his hand to the glass port. Their hands met through it.

"No," she said.

"Yes," he said. "Count me through. Four in. Hold. Four out. I will meet you at Point Twelve. Thirty breaths behind you."

Theta checked the panel. He shook his head.

"Go," Zane said. "They will spin the fallback on this corridor and they will take my name first."

Elia's vision narrowed. She set her mouth and gave him the only control she had.

"Four in," she said.

He matched her through the glass. "Hold."

"Four out."

He smiled with his mouth. His eyes stayed fierce. "I'm coming."

Mireya hauled Elia by the strap. "He bought the turn. You waste it if you stand."

Elia moved because he had moved first. Theta ran with her, hand still on the plate to steady the carrier through the corner. The corridor curved into a service bay that opened to a freight lift. Theta jammed it live with a blade tip. The lift crawled. The affect tone swung to resignation. Elia heard it and cut it with breath and a hard, clean anger that did not scatter her aim.

They rose into a maintenance deck that smelled of wet concrete and hot belts. Panels in the ceiling rattled from drones above. Mireya checked the landing. "Clear." She set pace through a toolroom and across a short run of catwalk.

Theta kept the carrier steady. Elia felt the cartridge in her pack settle at her spine and add mass to the choice they had made at the node.

They hit the western service spine. The seam Carrow had logged as a bypass stood unlocked. No gifts followed it.

The next door stayed shut. Mireya bridged the contacts with stripped wire and gave Elia a doorway and a count.

"Twenty breaths to Point 12," she said. "Three turns. Two cameras. One beam. Use the stingy corner on the second turn."

Elia moved. Weapon slung. Pack tight. Theta cut the first camera with a loop of tape and a mirror edge. Mireya threw the second off with a floor-shine that misreported heat. Theta brushed Elia's arm at the bend; the band beeped. She took more distance and broke the pair spike.

They entered the antechamber from the west. No guards. The tone rose for a hit that didn't come. They had outrun the model by a turn. Elia crossed the center without drama and gave the tower a short line built for people, not machines.

"You can stand," she said into the carrier. "You can stand with someone you trust while it hurts. Four in. Hold. Four out. Keep that count."

◄◄ ► ❚❚ ■ ►►

On Aric's wall the ring reshaped. Control collapsed into a waveform—a chest refusing to flatten. A tech named it out loud. Aric told the room to stabilize. The line wobbled and held.

◄◄ ► ❚❚ ■ ►►

Mireya cut the channel. "They know where we are," she said. "We go."

The freight stair dropped to a water-stained corridor and a heavy hatch. Theta found the pattern in the rust and set his palm where the hinge hid the latch. It gave. They slid into a service tunnel toward the old tram spur two blocks west. Damp air moved through it. A run of crew prints from winter repairs. One print from last week. Elia didn't spend a thought on it. She thought about the door with Zane's hand on the glass and the count in his mouth.

The tunnel kinked. The last hatch needed two bodies. Elia took the lower dogs. Mireya took the top. Theta shoved on the turn. The hatch released and swung. They spilled into a dim substation room with a stair to street level. Rain moved across the top grate in strips. The city's tone shifted.

FALLBACK_LATTICE: READY

AFFECT_VECTOR: CALM FALSE ↑

It wanted quiet streets for Cleanse. The command brushed Elia's jaw the way a hand tries to turn a head. She kept her face forward and climbed.

They reached the grate. Mireya tested the hinge. Stuck. She cut the bolt. They pushed. Rain fell through on their faces. Metal on the tongue. Elia stepped into it and let the air rinse the building off her.

Her comm ticked. Zane's voice came through thin with interference and still his.

"Point 12," he said. "Twenty behind. Hold the line."

"I've got his trail," Kade said, voice tight. "You run. I'll mark Point 12 and pull him through if the corridor loosens."

"Copy," she said.

The line crackled. Silence followed. The model ate the channel or the building did. She stood under the rain and let it fill her ears. She set her hand to the pack and felt the weight of the Origin and the fragment. She measured their next move against what they still held.

Mireya read the map in her head and found the next artery.

"We cut through Bracken," she said. "We string two more analogs. We open the mouth at the plaza. We make them listen. If he breaks through, he meets us there."

Elia nodded. She looked down the street. Cleanse trucks rolled three blocks east. People folded on benches. Bands pulsed amber. A boy crouched by a doorway with his hand on his sister's shoe so she would not get taken while she slept.

"We move to the plaza," Elia said. "We hold the count for them until they can hold it themselves."

Theta checked the carrier. It held steady. Mireya checked the rifle. It had rounds. Elia checked her breath. It did its job. She took the street with rain on her face and purpose in her step.

Behind them, a blast door groaned. A pin bent. A shoulder forced space where space had closed. A man in a jacket with a new wrap on one arm pulled through a gap and rose. Metal and copper on his tongue. Next task loaded. He set his jaw and went to find the people he had chosen.

Elia didn't look back. She didn't need to. She set the next turn and aimed them at Prime Core. She would finish the thing they had started and bring him through with the count still in his mouth.

REMEMBER AMERICA

The compound breathed again. Not on a schedule. Not by command. Fans turned. Stone held cool. Hands had warmed the room and left that heat in it. The archive stopped pretending to be a closet. Cables ran true into racks scarred by old labels. A legal oil lamp threw a thumb of flame. Elia sat on the floor where the sound behaved and pressed Record.

Resistance Archive

Entry one

"My name is Elia Ward. I remember."

She spoke the work the city had made her do and the work she chose after. She kept verbs hard and sentences plain. She set down where they stood and where they would go. The fragment pulsed under its glass. It did not lead. It listened.

Boots paused in the doorway. Theta had learned to step without warning the room. He nodded once, then gave her the thing he carried.

"Trace shows Zane's last mark at the aqueduct tower in nine," he said. "Outside the collapse."

"I'm still on the west analog," Kade said from the doorway, rain on his shoulders. "If he breathes, I'll hear it first."

Her chest tightened. She set the tightness in a corner and made space for air. "Outside gives him a path," she said.

Mireya stood behind Theta with wet hair and bright math in her eyes. "Not you," she said. "You're the archive. We lose you, we lose the map."

"If he breathes, we bring him home," Elia said. She did not turn the sentence into a hope. She wrote it as a task.

They left. The quiet folded back. Work filled the chairs by the crate. Three new faces took the circle. One wore grease under his nails that time would never scrub. One smelled of training oil. One kept a thin notebook and called himself a poet with a tremor he tried to hide.

Elia opened a box of what they had saved. Photos with burned corners. Clippings with edges that still cut. A page with a cornbread recipe in a hand that knew pleasure.

"This is the curriculum now," she said.

A boy sounded out a word from a clipping. "Baseball?"

"It was how we argued without losing each other," she said. "It smelled of summer. It carried home."

The girl touched the recipe. "This reads like my grandmother's kitchen."

"How do you smell paper," the drone trainee asked.

"You already do," Elia said.

The compound bent toward a new center. Above them the city changed its habits. Bands shed amber in strips. A street vendor peeled apples and handed wedges to strangers. A cook dug potatoes from dirt instead of gel and smiled when heat met taste. Children drew suns on doors and did not hide the chalk.

Three nights passed. Mireya came in out of the rain with a cloth-wrapped spike. She placed it on the table the way you lay a name down.

"He rerouted the last burst at the tower," she said. "Bought seconds for your drop. The drone cluster took the crown. We found this in the housing."

Elia slotted the spike. The screen woke to wind and night. Zane stood on the aqueduct platform with his shoulder burned and his mouth set. He worked wires with calm hands. The spike rode his teeth for a beat while he stripped a lead, then he drove it home.

"Count my breaths," he said into rain. He threw a breaker. Light guttered. A scout beam found steel, not skin. He laughed once. Another beam cut in from the east. He struck a flare and rolled it out. Heat rose. "Eight," he counted, steady. "Seven."

White smeared the lens. The picture came back to his weight on one knee, blood in a run behind him. He jammed a final lead, set his brow to metal in a brief bow. "For you," he said, and worked.

The feed tore to static. The tower crown flared in red. Rain turned to steam. The platform stood empty.

Mireya stopped the clip. No one spoke. Elia set her palm on the cloth and kept her face plain. "Thank you," she said to the dead channel.

Theta watched the live stream on a second screen. The model wrote fresh red at the edges they held. "Fallback lattice spins in Prime," he said. "Sanctum still pulls power through scaffold."

"Then cut scaffold," Mireya said. "We don't rally a crowd. We don't have bodies to waste. We have a voice." Elia looked at the fragment and at the cassette they had pulled from the throat of the tower.

AXIOM: ORIGIN VOICE / SEED

Stamped the case. She kept her voice level.

"We climb the skywalk spine. We hang analog across bone. We carry Origin on the coil. No tape. Me." She faced Theta. "You hold the carrier when the system starts to grind. Mireya holds the line. If the tone starts to teach us to behave, cut it and bring it back to me."

They moved through a corridor Carrow had kept on his key. The reader swallowed a badge without fuss. A door shrugged. A stair rose with bad paint and rust that bit. Theta carried the case as if it weighed the same as a friend. Mireya kept the ugly rifle she never apologized for. Elia slung cable and water.

They climbed. At the hatch the wind met them full. The skywalk stack held old metal and new tension. Mireya fired grapples into swollen struts, then hung her weight on each and grunted when they held. Theta married Origin to the mast. Elia set the fragment to teach the coil without burning it. She taped the mic to ridgeline and stood with her scarf at her throat.

A step at the hatch. Carrow stood half in shadow. No pistol in his hand. A small device in his palm.

"You mean to speak," he said. "You need thirty breaths. If you stop at twenty-nine, Sanctum runs a kill script. If you cross thirty, the loop trips and eats its own feet."

"Carrier's yours," Kade said into Elia's cuff. "Thirty clean if you hold the line."

Mireya raised one brow. "No charge. That your new habit."

"I'm late to this faith," he said to Elia. "Your mother bet on you. I signed a waiver and called it courage. Hold me to something better."

Theta marked the device with his eye. "If you stay, you burn."

"If I run, I still burn," Carrow said, and held the hatch.

Theta opened his hand. "On you," he said to Elia. He set fingers to knobs. Numbers moved in his head.

Elia tightened the scarf. She placed her mouth to the mic. The first second fought her body. The second fell into place. She spoke and did not dress it.

"Neighbors. Children. My name is Elia Ward. The static that spoke to you carried my breath. They built Harmony from it. They named that theft peace. They taught you to call forgetting health. They told you error when you remembered a face, a song, a taste. That feeling in your throat at night is grief. You live with it in company. You heal with it in company."

Sanctum pushed tone through the wire. Theta nudged the carrier. "Three," he said under his breath. "Four."

Elia kept her cadence clean. "Stand with someone you trust. If fear sits beside you, breathe with me. Four in. Hold. Four out. Hold. Keep that count until your thoughts stop marching where you did not send them."

In a kitchen, a woman set her band on a table and left it there. On a bench a man wrote his child's name until the paper refused more ink. A boy pinned a drawing to a post and did not hide it under a bed.

The coil lifted hair on their arms. Theta gripped the plate and kept the tone from clawing through. "Eight," he said. "Nine."

Mireya watched the stair through steady sight. She breathed on four and did not blink when movement shifted at the edge.

Kade fee the feed from Sector 9, "Singal holds. Your voice is across 9. It's in the ears, Elia."

Elia spoke through that movement.

"I loved a man," she said. "He bought us seconds. I spend them now. If you hold a second, spend it. Hoarding time serves the system that starved you."

"Thirteen," Theta said. Carrow turned the first pair away with authority and shrug. He stepped into the third and broke a wrist clean. The man folded. Carrow closed the hatch and held it with his back.

"Fifteen," Theta said. The tone bored into bone. Elia felt a nail at the base of her skull and kept her jaw loose.

"We lived before the grid. We will live after. Your grandmother's recipe is a map. Your brother's song in the dark is law. Your child's star on a door is constitution. Sign it when you pass."

"Twenty-one." The wire sang. "Twenty-two." Mireya put a man down and did not waste a second on pride. "Twenty-three."

"Soldiers on the east stair," Carrow said through his teeth. "Two I can turn. Not three."

"Twenty-four." Heat built at the mast. The scarf snapped at Elia's neck. She did not step back.

"Carrow," she said without looking. "Hold the door until it bites."

"I hold," he said.

"Twenty-seven," Theta said. His palm smoked at the edge. "Twenty-eight."

Elia did not say America. She said, "We remember."

"Twenty-nine."

Sanctum armed the cut. Carrow's device buzzed. He moved his thumb from authorized to delay and pressed. "Thirty," Theta said, stunned and glad. "You're across."

The system did what systems do when a script fails. It threw fire. A thin white arc climbed the mast. Metal brightened to a color with no name. The scarf at Elia's throat flared blue, then burned. Theta smashed the cut switch. The knob thunked. Heat already lived in the steel. Elia took one more breath and finished.

"They taught forgetting as peace. Remembering is power. I remember."

The current took her. Light ran her arm and shoulder and throat and threw her back into the rail. The mic popped and spat. Theta pulled her clear. He pressed his ear to her mouth. Wind filled it. He found her wrist and counted because she had given him a count.

"One," he said. Nothing. "Two." Nothing. "Three."

Mireya set a patch and knew it would not change the math. She said Elia's name and held the head she had not allowed herself to touch before. Theta felt a small tremor die under his thumb. He closed her eyes. No theater. Only respect.

The rig hissed itself quiet. The city tilted toward stillness the way a crowd tilts before it sings. Carrow took a step and stopped, jaw hard.

Word ran through stair and hall and vent. She did it. She's gone. She did it.

They worked through grief. That room did not permit ceremony to swallow labor. Someone gathered the coil bones. Theta carried the recorder down and set it on the crate where Elia had sat. He pressed Record because ritual holds.

Mireya leaned into the mic.

Resistance Archive

Entry two.

"My name is Mireya. I remember."

Theta added his name without pause. **Resistance Archive**

Entry two (addendum).

"My name is Theta. I remember choosing."

Resistance Archive

Entry three.

"My name is Kade," he said to the mic, voice rough. "I remember calling windows and you walking through."

The boy with the notebook stepped in with empty hands. "I remember a song I don't know yet," he said. No one corrected him. A woman read a recipe with her whole face soft. The drone trainee said baseball and held the room steady through its laugh and its tears. They said I remember. The room learned its own chorus.

Carrow stood in the doorway and spoke a name as order and prayer. He placed his device in Theta's palm. "You have thirty every time now," he said. "Waste them better." He bowed his head to the lamp and left before anyone made him a clean story.

Across the city, bands turned to ash on wrists. Windows opened. Faces leaned into wet air. A vendor cut apples and pressed wedges into hands. The cook broke a potato with both thumbs and sent the bowl down a line. Children chased chalk suns down a stair. Men and women shouted names into hall wells and no one fined them.

On the roof, wind moved through the char and left a hush. Theta stood there alone and set his hand to the mast. The metal still held a faint hum. He nodded to nothing and honored it.

In the streets, people tested a word. They put it on doors and paper and palms. They folded it into napkins and birds and tucked it into pockets. They taught it at bedsides. They held it on their tongues until mouths remembered how to shape it without fear.

The lamp in the archive guttered and caught again. The recorder's red eye blinked. They packed the coil bones in a box. Theta wrote with the stub of pencil:

WARD — CALDER (sealed)

Above, a girl on a roof set a fiddle under her chin and drew two notes. The metal answered. She laughed and turned to her mother. "Do you hear it?"

"I do," her mother said. "Say it."

"I remember," the girl whispered. The wind carried it to a window. Another mouth caught it. The word moved block to block. A woman at a sink wiped her hands and leaned out and spoke it. A man on a stoop raised a wedge of apple and toasted it. A boy at a stair called it into the well.

Voices caught and built and did not stop.

"We—"

Windows swung wide. A pan rang. A ladle struck a pot. A bow drew a long line.

"—re—"

Feet found rhythm. Hands met hands.

"—mem—"

The sound rolled into the avenues and up the towers and down the rails. It touched the rooms where the bands lay in little drifts and did not wake them.

"—ber!"

The city answered itself, loud and alive and unafraid.

"WE REMEMBER AMERICA."

THE QUIET REBUILD

Stars spilled over the city like nails on black cloth. Ivy climbed the lattice. Moss took the mouths of dead drones. An old turbine turned and made plain power. Market tarps snapped. Onion hit hot oil. Rain lifted stone smell from broken streets. Music rose from throats and strings and a boy's wire guitar with one sharp note that made the corner grin.

People changed their walk. Shoulders dropped. Lines formed for oranges no one could prove were real. A child drew a star, then a shape that wasn't a star, and laughed. Men opened radios, gutted the old silence, found a bed of static that belonged to no one. Voices slid in: a grandmother's lullaby in the outlaw tongue; a worker reporting the river at first light; a girl telling how bread that tasted like dirt made her cry.

In a tunnel room with bad echo, Mireya took chalk and a class. She wrote dates. She made kids wipe and write again. "You're not memorizing," she said. "You're remembering." A boy who had turned drones with a visor read a paragraph about baseball as if it might break. "That's how we argued," someone said from the back, and the laugh that came after it felt earned. A girl held a cornbread recipe. "This smells like my grandmother's house." When a kid asked how paper could carry a smell, she lifted her chin. "It does." The room went still and kept that truth.

Theta worked ground and wire. A repaired transformer hummed where it had learned to sag. He logged rotation on a wall ledger: beans, then wheat, then potatoes after frost. He soldered two lengths of copper over the guts of an old radio and listened to the clean fit. Someone had painted PROJECT EDEN on a school wall. He said the name was dumb and wrote it on the next crate anyway. At dusk he tuned a counter-hum into the kids' hour and cracked a lullaby sweep in half. Children read poems and snorted with it. He grinned and set the level by thumb.

STATIC

RELAY LIVE

The comms cracked, "This is Kade. Sector 9 relay open. Resistance Archive holds."

Carrow pulled two fuses in a stairwell and wrote the failure up with a straight face. He reclassified one panel to safety check and let a door forget to close. He carried a box of dog-eared files to a woman with dirt under her nails.

"These belong to your house," he said.

She found a name inside and set her jaw like a person who had found a lost bone.

"Leave before I thank you."

He passed two of his own men on the stairs. No one spoke.

In a clean basement a few coats stood over a table and a black rectangle. A schematic glowed. It did not look like a tower. It looked like a fever.

"Memory made unbearable," a man said.

"They will beg us for the cold." A woman with gray at the temples said,

"It won't work on children." He tapped the device. "We never build for children. We build for the ones who teach them." No one said the old name.

The people's ribs on the roofs threw a new weather. A widow told how she sat on the floor and ate jam with her fingers after the knock because a spoon felt like a ceremony she couldn't stand.

Two teenagers argued on air about the word *revolution* and then laughed at themselves and kept arguing. In a dead training hall a boy propped a patched player on a console and ran a clip. The wall gave back a voice the room had been built to hate: *They told us forgetting was peace. But remembering... that's power.* He ran down the corridor and yelled for his friends. No one stopped him. In the archive, a reel on a shelf wore a neat label in Theta's hand:

WARD — CALDER (sealed)

On a roof at Sector 5 a coil stub, five buttons, and a shard of glass made a small shrine. No photo. The city kept that sort of thing in its chest.

Mireya touched the coil with the back of her hand. "Keep your stupid promises, you handsome idiot."

The wind moved the line along. On the western rib a rumor took root: set a mug on the iron, press your ear to rust, hear a pattern. A kid tried it at noon like a dare. Wind. Then not wind. Short, short, long. A space. Long, long, short. His skin lifted. He went home and counted thirty with his mother at the sink and felt ready for a thing he could not name.

Theta woke to a sweep that walked block to block and pressed the same breath on every chest. He tuned a wobble into the children's slot and set it loose. Two lines met. The edge snapped off the lullaby. He laughed at an empty ceiling. "You don't own the song."

Freedom did not fix the floor. It made work possible. Men with rubber boots carried seed on a factory line and learned dirt by hand. Water hit warm plates and steamed.

A woman spoke into a tin comm: "Rotation holds. Compost black. Eden until someone finds a better joke."

"Copy" a voice said and meant it.

On a Thursday, a room full of broken chairs a midwife taught care as craft and wrote births in a book.

"What do we call this feeling," a boy asked her.

"Alive," she said.

The room didn't laugh.

Enemies learned patience. Faces with no uniform met under good lights and built a rumor machine.

"We don't rebuild the grid," a thin voice said. "We rebuild obedience."

Fingers traced a new device and gave it an easy name that tasted like ash in the mouth. They planned a sweep with sugar on it.

Night came without sirens. Lamps bent their necks. Radio ribs warmed. Chalk suns spread down a stair. Pots knocked lids. Hands wrote names on walls in charcoal and left them for morning.

The outlands held a darker dark. A signal post stood on a ridge scratched with a cradle mark—two lines crossed, neat and plain. A radio woke, stuttered, smoothed. Static clumped. Under it, a voice:

"Count my breaths."

Distance chewed the edges. The cadence still carried.

Another voice answered on the next break. Not an ending. A habit.

"Always."

A scarred hand set a small stone at the post. Elia clipped a battered relay to the rig. The burn at her wrist caught starlight. Zane shouldered a pack and checked the tether twice. He looked toward the sleeping grid of streets.

"The Choir first," she said.

"We make the thirty," he said.

Boots whispered through grass. Two shadows took the slope and drew one line toward work. The ribs on the roofs ticked like cooling engines. Somewhere a child counted to four and slept. Somewhere a ledger waited for a name. Somewhere, under the new quiet, a voice kept playing. And someone kept listening.

From
Gingerbread
Publishing House

COMING 2026

www.ingramcontent.com/pod-product-compliance
Lightning Source LLC
Chambersburg PA
CBHW030758200726
PP18592100001B/7